Now, Rick and Evie must hop aboard their hovership and travel across the world to locate a special vine that will allow them to anchor their beloved paradise to the Earth's crust.

But the Lanes better pick up the pace. If they're even a second late, everything that they built will go **POW LIKE PANGAEA!**

"How could this even happen?" Evie fumed. "It's a continent! It's not like Europe *goes for a swim* every now and then."

Dad tried to explain. "Honey, the eighth continent isn't like Earth's other landmasses. It's made of converted trash, which was floating on the surface of the water."

"That means that the continent we created also floats *on top* of the water," Rick clarified.

"Will the eighth continent be okay?"

Rick shook his head. "We wanted there to be eight continents, but if we can't stop ours from crashing into Australia, there will only be six."

PRAISE FOR **THE 8TH CONTINENT** SERIES:

"**Fast-paced action**, cool inventions and remarkable robots combine for an auspicious opener."

—*Kirkus Reviews*

"**Good fun** in the tradition of M. T. Anderson's Pals in Peril series."

—*Booklist*

"**Zippy pace** and **original premise**."

—*School Library Journal*

"London's **smart and humorous** series launch hurtles along at a . . . knuckle-whitening pace. Kids will especially enjoy George's outlandish robotic and vehicular inventions—including 2-Tor, the siblings' giant mechanical crow teacher—in this fun yet thought-provoking story."

—*Publishers Weekly*

"This is a delightful start to the adventures of the Lane family, with their flying tree and their mechanical bird tutor. Evie and Rick and their brilliant if eccentric parents are **wonderfully vivid**, and the villains who try to impede them in their quest to save the Earth, equally **memorable.** It's all in the great tradition of adventure fiction for young readers, running back through Akiko and Freddy the Pig all the way to Tom Sawyer."

—Kim Stanley Robinson, author of *Red Mars*

MATT LONDON

An Imprint of Penguin Group (USA)

THE
8TH
CONTINENT
WELCOME TO THE JUNGLE
BUILD IT.
RUN IT.
RULE IT.
MATT LONDON

For my family

A division of Penguin Young Readers Group
Published by the Penguin Group
Penguin Group (USA) LLC
345 Hudson Street
New York, New York 10014

USA / Canada / UK / Ireland / Australia / New Zealand
India / South Africa / China
Penguin.com
A Penguin Random House Company

ISBN: 978-1-59514-755-4

Printed in the United States of America

1 3 5 7 9 10 8 6 4 2

"SOMETHING TELLS ME THEY'RE NOT HERE TO WELCOME US TO THE NEIGHBORHOOD."

Evie Lane squinted, trying to count the number of robots racing through the ocean toward her family's new home, the eighth continent. There were hundreds of them, row after row of birds and beasts and sea monsters that stretched back to the horizon. It looked like the whole zoo had attended swimming lessons, then escaped, taken a detour through a pink-paint factory, then another detour through a turn-you-into-a-robot factory, and now were after revenge.

"Something tells me they're not here to help us build, either."

That was Rick, Evie's older brother by one year, who was a total nerd, but a cool nerd. Evie had decided this because when she and Rick were racing all over the world trying to create the eighth continent, they saved each other's lives five or six times, and now they were a pretty good team. Like when Evie said something like, "Holy smoked salmon! That's a lot of robots!" Rick would say something like, "According to my calculations they'll be here in six seconds." And then at the exact same moment they would realize these hot-pink robots weren't just something conceptual to discuss and analyze, but were actively trying to mangle, maul, and masticate the duo. And then they'd leap, often literally, into action.

"Something tells me we should run! Quick children, to the *Roost*!"

That was Dad—more famously known as George Lane, the President of Lane Industries, and the super-genius inventor of the hover engine, the Eden Compound, talking robots, and the turkey caramel sandwich (don't ask).

Prior to the arrival of the unwanted robot intruders, the Lane family had been sitting around a campfire on the shore of the eighth continent, debating what to name their new home. It was hard to believe that what was now a fertile landmass larger than Madagascar had been a reeking pile of floating garbage in the Pacific Ocean just six weeks earlier. Thanks, however, to Dad's trash-transformation formula—the Eden Compound—the Lane siblings had successfully converted the Great Pacific Garbage Patch, as the pile of floating garbage had been called, into a beautiful paradise, the first new continent in fifty million years.

But now there was no time for toasting marshmallows and reminiscing. Still clutching their barbeque skewers, the Lanes turned and ran, desperate to escape from the oncoming pink army. Following closely behind was Mom Lane, given name Melinda, known at Cleanaspot, the global soap manufacturing company she managed, as "Boss Lady." And known in the Lane household as "Boss Lady." (There were few places where she wasn't known as Boss Lady.) At Mom's side was the Lanes' formerly robotic seven-foot-tall crow instructor, 2-Tor—named as such for reasons Evie could never really remember, though she suspected it had something to do with her dad just throwing random words together until he found an acronym that sounded like tutor.

"I say, go away!" 2-Tor flapped his sleek black wings at the approaching robot army, his spindly talons digging into the spongy terrain as he made his way across the continent.

Unfortunately, this did nothing to deter the hundreds of oncoming robots. Mechanical bears surged from the water. Tigers and other sharp-toothed predators flooded the shore. The animals charged onto the beach, red robo-eyes burning furiously. As Evie sprinted, keeping pace with the rest of her family, she noticed each of these vicious machines had a television in its stomach, just like 2-Tor. On each fluorescent screen was the wicked, cackling face of Evie's schoolmate/personal nightmare, Vesuvia Piffle. Vesuvia was the super-secret CEO of the voracious real-estate development group Condo Corp, a company whose shady business practices made everyone wonder if they were just regular evil, or the kind of evil that only comes from being run by a self-obsessed eleven-year-old.

Or was it former CEO? Evie wasn't sure. After the Battle of the Garbage Patch, when Evie and Rick had used the

Eden Compound to create the eighth continent, Vesuvia had been arrested by Winterpole and sent to the Prison at the Pole. But if Vesuvia was locked up, then who was controlling the robot army?

From the screens, Vesuvia screeched, "I've got you now, Lane-sers. That's like 'Losers,' but with your name! HAHAHAHAHAHAHA!"

A flock of robo-birds roared overhead. Their beaks opened and big globs of a chunky white substance shot out. Evie skipped over a glob that splatted at her feet. "Cottage cheese?"

"Who knows?" Rick said, taking her hand. "Run!"

At the base of a nearby hill, they reached the *Roost*. The hovership was standing upright on its roots, its engines gray and cold. It was the closest the Lanes' flying machine ever came to looking like the giant sequoia tree it had been before being knocked down by a lightning strike and turning into Rick and Evie's primary means of transportation.

An entry tube emerged from under the roots of the hovership, and the four Lanes and 2-Tor were slurped inside like action figures into a power-vacuum. They scrambled through the narrow corridors and into their seats on the bridge. Without warning, Dad kicked the throttle up to full and rocketed the ship into the air.

The little pink birds collided with the *Roost*'s windshield like hailstones as Dad tried to gain height. One broke clean through the glass and embedded itself in the command console, sending up a shower of sparks. Evie recoiled in surprise, stumbling into her mother, who held her tight.

"Oh no!" Rick pointed out the window. "Dad, look out!"

A trio of robo-vultures were clutching an enormous pink giraffe in their talons, and they were getting ready to fling it at the *Roost*. The vultures let go and Dad yanked the *Roost* sideways, narrowly missing the long-necked machine flying at them like a tomahawk.

"We can't keep this up forever!" Dad mourned. The vultures were already hoisting a robo-hippopotamus into the air. It was hard to tell who looked less pleased, the birds or the hippo.

Evie rubbed her temples, trying to think of ideas, but she only came up with one. "Rick!" she shouted across the roaring cockpit. "Got any ideas?"

"Maybe! Dad, where'd you put that old squid-cuff Winterpole used to lock you up?"

"Squid-cuff . . ." Mom repeated, sounding confused. "This is hardly the time!"

"Trust me!" Rick insisted.

Dad barked quick directions to the squid-cuff's location in the storage hold.

"Got it!" Rick yelled, dashing out the door faster than if he'd heard the electronics store was giving away free video games. Evie followed, cheering, "Plan! Plan! We have a plan!"

As his sister reached the storage hold, Rick dropped to his knees and skidded halfway across the varnished wood floor. He slid to a stop in front of a large plastic bucket surrounded by old rags. Rolling up his sleeves, Rick jammed his hands into the bucket, sloshing neon-blue fluid over the rim. He carefully pulled out a limp cybernetic tentacle. LEDs blinked underneath its translucent skin.

Rick hurried past Evie, squid-cuff in hand. "Quick, we gotta get to the balcony."

They ran across the catwalk over the engine room, but as they reached the door to the balcony, something vast struck the side of the *Roost*. The hovership spiraled on its central axis, spinning over and over like a barrel rolling down a hill. Evie and Rick grabbed the catwalk railing, their insides doing somersaults as the ship attempted to regain equilibrium.

At last the hovership righted itself and the kids burst onto the balcony. Wind rushed past Evie's ears and blew her hair wild. The squid-cuff flapped in Rick's hands, its tentacles wriggling.

The sky was filled with flying robots. Robo-birds carpet bombed the continent with spoiled foodstuffs until the land's surface looked like a forgotten casserole in the back of a refrigerator. Some of the more colossal machines took to the air on spinning propellers, slamming into the hull of the *Roost* in an effort to bring it down.

"Okay, Rick, we're here," Evie said. "Now what do we do?"

"Right!" Rick grinned, holding the squid-cuff away from his face. "Remember what happened when 2-Tor got too close to this thing?"

"How could I forget? He set off the EMP inside the

squid-cuff. His malfunctioning almost crashed the *Roost*!"

"Exactly." Rick nodded. "2-Tor was a robot at the time, and the electromagnetic pulse inside this squid-cuff seriously damaged his vital systems on contact. Soooo . . ."

Evie perked up. "Soooo . . . if we hit a robot with the squid-cuff now, it'll short it out."

"Correct! Assuming all these robots are network-linked, this should shut the whole thing down. Now stand back, I'm going to throw it."

"Wait, wait, wait." Evie held his arm. "*You* are going to throw it?"

Both kids ducked as a fanged robo-bunny whizzed over their heads. "Of course I'm going to throw it," Rick said, rising to his feet. "It was my idea."

"Oh, right." Evie rolled her eyes. "I forgot you have a gold medal in Olympic squid throwing."

"You don't think I can do it?" Rick sounded offended.

"That's not true!" Evie smirked playfully. "I *know* you can't do it."

While Rick and Evie bickered, an enormous robo-shark rose to eye level. Its metal exoskeleton was hot pink. A wide hover engine had been grafted to the robot's belly, allowing it to keep pace with the *Roost*. Its hinged jaw opened wide, revealing several rows of whirring chainsaw teeth.

It was at that moment that Evie noticed the shark. "It's Chompedo! Look out!" she cried, grabbing the squid-cuff from Rick. She threw it at Vesuvia Piffle's most beloved robot. The robo-shark swallowed the squid-cuff whole.

Nothing happened. Evie and Rick held their breath.

Suddenly, currents of electricity surged over Chompedo like a tiny dancing lightning storm. His eyes sparked. His teeth stopped whirring. His entire body reeled.

Rick smacked the call button on the comm box next to the door leading back into the *Roost*. "Dad! Hard right! Now!"

The *Roost* lurched, pulling away from Chompedo. The lightbulbs behind the shark's red eyes popped. A tremendous shockwave flew from its body.

Rick and Evie stared in stone silence. Then the shockwave overtook the other robots. The Lanes watched in amazement as members of the Piffle fleet started shaking, their charred pink exoskeletons breaking open.

"It worked! I was right!" Rick pumped his fists and shook his hips. Evie tried not to giggle.

But then the shockwave reversed, and Evie felt the *Roost* being pulled toward Chompedo.

"What's going on?" Her voice quaked with fear.

Rick grabbed on to the communicator box to anchor himself. He pushed the talk button to send a message to his parents on the bridge. "Dad! Dad! The interaction between the shark and the squid-cuff must have created a powerful electromagnet. It's going to pull us in!"

"Roger that!" Dad's voice chirped over the communicator. The *Roost* shook as he kicked in the afterburners, moving them away from the shark magnet.

The other robots' engines weren't strong enough to fight

the draw of the magnet. The robo-vultures, giraffes, and other animals were being yanked toward the shark, forming a huge ball of mangled pink metal around Chompedo. They held there for a second and Evie felt her breath catch in her throat. "Did we do it?" she whispered.

The lump of magnetized robots plummeting to the ground answered her question a moment later.

"Wahoo!" Evie cheered. "We disabled their engines. Smart thinking, Rick. That'll teach those pink pests."

Rick leaned over the side of the balcony to keep the robots in sight. "Thanks, but this is nothing to wahoo about. According to my calculations, the robots' current speed and trajectory will make them crash into—oh no!"

"'Oh no!?'" Evie wailed. "'Oh no' is a terrible place to crash!"

The words were barely out of her mouth before the robots struck the edge of the eighth continent.

The shockwave from the impact was so intense it nearly rattled the *Roost* apart. Evie gripped the balcony railing to hold it and herself steady. She looked over the edge, prepared for the sight of a big crater in her beloved homeland. What she saw, however, was even worse:

The continent *moved*.

Evie wiped her eyes, sure that they were deceiving her. But, no, there was the continent, skipping across the ocean like a stone across a pond. Then it started to drift south, caught in a powerful ocean current.

"Uh, did you just see that?" Evie asked, her face ashen.

Rick just stood there speechless. Then finally he said, "So that's what 'oh no' looks like."

A few minutes later Rick and Evie finished recounting this latest development to their parents up on the bridge. "How could this even happen?" Evie fumed. "It's a continent! It's not like Europe *goes for a swim* every now and then."

Dad tried to explain. "Honey, the eighth continent isn't like earth's other landmasses. It's made of converted trash, which was floating on the surface of the water."

"That means that the continent we created also floats on the water, all loosey-goosey," Rick clarified.

"But a floating continent isn't our problem," Dad added. "It's the fact that since it's been set adrift, it could hit other landmasses and completely disrupt oceanographic stability."

"That sounds bad," Evie said.

"Very bad." Rick nodded, examining the *Roost*'s global positioning system. "Based on the eighth continent's current trajectory, it will collide with Australia in two days."

Mom turned white. "What kind of mess will that make?"

Rick looked at her, his eyes filled with fear. "I can't predict the extent of the damage, but 'catastrophic' is a word that comes to mind."

"Will the eighth continent be okay?" Evie asked worriedly.

Rick shook his head. "We wanted there to be eight continents, but if we can't stop ours from crashing into Australia, there will only be six."

DIANA MAPLE'S FOOTSTEPS FELL LIKE RAINDROPS AS SHE RACED THROUGH THE FRIGID HALLWAYS of Winterpole Headquarters. She still felt uncomfortable in her new junior-agent uniform. The waist was sewn so tight she could barely breathe, and the black collar constricted her throat. But she would never admit any of this to her mother.

Mrs. Maple walked a few steps ahead of Diana. Her chic black hair remained frozen in a perfect bob despite the speediness of her stride. As usual, Diana found it hard to keep up. It had been her mother's idea to enroll Diana in Winterpole's junior-agent program, an internship that let kids prepare for an exciting career in eco-protection enforcement. Except *exciting* meant *mind-numbing*, and *career* meant *paperwork*.

Despite her misgivings, Diana was not about to refuse an offer of employment at Winterpole. Her former boss and best friend, Vesuvia Piffle, had been locked up by the international rule-makers; and Diana's mother, a high-ranking

Winterpole agent, had barely looked at her daughter since Vesuvia's incarceration.

Diana's lungs seized up whenever she thought about her mother's diamond-hard glare. That judgmental shake of her head. Diana didn't want to give her mom or anyone else reason to suspect she was still on Vesuvia's side.

As they reached the end of a long corridor, Diana's mother opened a set of heavy steel doors and the two Maple women stepped through. The room beyond was vast and rectangular with a high arched roof. Every surface—walls, ceiling, and floor—was covered with blocks of icy-blue metal. In the center of the room was a desk made of deep blue stone, and on it was an enormous flatscreen monitor, which displayed the bald head of an older gentleman. But the face wasn't a video as much a representation, lines of code that bent and danced as the visage moved. This indirect and unsettling method of communication was the Director of Winterpole's preferred way of dictating instructions to his employees. Diana had never seen the Director in person, and neither had any of the other junior agents.

Both side walls of the Director's office were lined with risers, formed of smooth-cut blocks of honest-to-goodness ice. "Sit," Diana's mother hissed, pulling her to a spot where they had a good view of the Director.

Diana winced as she sat down. The icy seat chilled her to the marrow.

Before the desk stood a man wearing the standard three-piece suit of a Winterpole agent. He had trim hair, dark except for streaks of white on both sideburns, and was in the middle of a presentation to the Director and the assembled audience. Diana knew him to be one of Winterpole's top operatives—and also the man who had made it his mission to arrest George Lane.

Mister Snow cleared his throat and continued speaking. "Approximately two hours ago, at oh-six-hundred Greenwich mean time, our aerial scanners detected an intercontinental collision. A pink UPO, or unidentified plummeting object, made impact on the surface of the landmass dubbed by the outlaw George Lane as 'the eighth continent.' This collision knocked the former garbage patch into a southern-trending ocean current, and now the continent is on a doomsday course for Australia. Estimated time of impact is in just under forty-six hours. We must intercept the eighth continent and arrest George Lane before it's too late."

When the Director replied, his voice was a dark and menacing mix of static and subwoofer. "Winterpole lacks jurisdiction beyond the seven continents. You know that, Snow. Every good agent knows that. Why would you bring me this information?"

"Yes, Director," Mister Snow bowed his head, "but do not forget Statute 76A-501—"

"I never forget a statute!" the Director snapped. "76A-501: when one landmass threatens another, Winterpole may intervene, regardless of jurisdiction. Agents! Activate the Winterpole Crisis Clause."

A high-pitched honking noise filled the air. Diana and some of the other junior agents covered their ears. Panels opened along the walls, and a gaggle of white geese spilled out like rats escaping a flooded subway tunnel. "HONK! HONK! HOOOOOOONK!" they screeched. The stampede of geese flooded into the halls, filling all of Winterpole Headquarters with noise.

Wincing, Diana looked at her mother. "Couldn't we come up with a more efficient alarm system?"

Diana's mother hushed her impatiently.

Straightening to his full height, Mister Snow smiled like he'd just won the world's creepiest lottery. "Mister Director, agents of Winterpole, now that the Crisis Clause has been activated, I must report a disturbing fact. George Lane has threatened the sovereign continent of Australia. We must intervene and legislate his illegal continent. George Lane must be taken into custody. He must be brought to the Prison at the Pole."

"You will assemble a team, Mister Snow." The Director sounded equally pleased. His digitized face grinned with satisfaction. "And good work."

Mister Snow bowed his head more deeply this time. *Were those tears in his eyes?* "Thank you, Director. I live to please you."

THE EIGHTH CONTINENT MOVED SOUTHWEST THROUGH THE PACIFIC OCEAN LIKE A TURTLE OF unimaginable size. Frothing white wake churned behind the former garbage patch in the shape of a V. Despite its great mass, the continent showed no sign of slowing down.

Neither did the Lane family. They had worked straight through until morning to come up with a way to stop the eighth continent from crashing into Australia.

Rick checked the Continent Collision Counter application he'd programmed on his family's pocket tablets to keep track of how much time they had left. Just two days were remaining. Their predicament irritated Rick so much he almost couldn't breathe. He had big plans for the eighth continent, plans he had spent the past six weeks preparing to execute. His frequent disagreements with Evie about what to do with their new homeland had set him back enough already. And a crisis like this didn't just mean more delays; it meant that he might never see his dream of a thoughtful and unencumbered civilization realized. But this wasn't even Rick's focus at the moment. He had only one clear thing driving him: he *had* to find a solution, or else they'd be saying g'night to the people who say g'day.

Rick's mind sparked and skittered with ideas as dawn rose over the Pacific horizon, casting bright sunlight across the gentle hills of the eighth continent. Standing outside his father's hastily constructed laboratory, he looked at the landscape he'd helped create. Dirt and rocks and grass stretched as far as the eye could see. A mountain range stood tall in the distance.

Those were the things the eighth continent had. What it didn't have yet were trees or leafy plants of any kind, and the only buildings were the small cluster of temporary wooden shelters his family had erected north of the beach.

"Koo ka-koo ka-KOO!!!" From the open front door of the lab, Dad called like a bird. It was a cry the family used at times when it was urgent to have everyone rally to the same location. "Rick! Come here. I think I have something."

Rick hurried inside, where his father was standing next to 2-Tor. The bird held a quilt-sized sheet of white paper in his beak and the tips of his outstretched wings.

Rick's dad scribbled something furiously, then stepped back to show Rick the plan. "If we construct a giant desk fan and mount it on the continent, we may be able to blow our runaway home off-course."

Rick glanced across the room where Mom and Evie were considering an idea of their own. Mom was drawing on a chalkboard while thinking out loud. "The continent is like a dog off its leash. Maybe we could order a fleet of my Cleanaspot mega-vacuums to rendezvous with it. If they were all sucking water at full power, they might be able to slurp us off-course."

"I don't know, Melinda. . . ." Dad piped up, looking over from the mess of scribbles on his paper. "Not a bad idea, but hmm . . . we need to get to the root of the problem."

It suddenly dawned on Rick that his father was right. "That's . . . that's it!" he exclaimed.

His family turned to him in confusion. "What's it?" Evie said.

"What Dad just said. We have to get to the *root* of the problem. By rooting the eighth continent!"

"Richard," 2-Tor interrupted, "I'm not sure what you took your father's meaning to be, but all he was suggesting was that—"

Rick cut his tutor off. "Mom hit on it too when she said the continent was like a dog off its leash." He looked at his mother in expectation but she just stared back at him blankly. Rick searched for a way to explain himself. "You guys all know that even if we could build a fan or a vacuum big enough to push us away from Australia, we'd still run the risk of getting stuck in another ocean current. We're floating ducks out here unless we stop the eighth continent from moving permanently, and the only way to do that is by *rooting* the continent to the ocean floor."

"Oh, I get it," said Dad. "That's genius, son!"

Mom's eyes widened. "Brilliant! That'll be the perfect way to avoid dirtying the oceans."

Evie raised a skeptical eyebrow. "Am I the only one here who still doesn't know what he's talking about?"

"Yes," said her parents in unison.

Rick snatched Dad's pen from his hand and started sketching his vision. "Think of the continent as a lily pad. We need to create a tether to connect it to the bottom of the ocean."

Rick's parents nodded in agreement as he spoke, making Rick swell with pride.

"The only issue will be finding a strong anchor that's long enough to hold a whole continent in place." He turned to his favorite crow. "2-Tor, how long will the root need to be?"

"The ocean floor at our current location is fourteen thousand feet below sea level."

"Well, that's not too far at all then, is it?" Dad exclaimed. "I think Rick may be on to something. Honey, what do you think? Is this a project Professor Doran could help us with?"

Rick's mother nodded. "Professor Doran! Now there's a fine idea."

Dad nodded in satisfaction. "Good. Kids, listen up. Professor Doran is an old friend of your mother's and mine. He's a prize-winning botanist who specializes in super plants. If anyone knows how to grow a root big enough to anchor the eighth continent, it's him. I'll take you to his lab in Texas, down on the Mexican border."

"Yee-haw!" Evie hooted. "We're going on another adventure."

"But Dad," Rick interjected. "You can't leave the eighth continent, or Winterpole will arrest you."

"Oh yeah, he's right," Evie agreed. "You can't go with us."

Rick's father seemed quite flustered by this inconvenience. "Hmm. Okay. Well then your mother will go with you. 2-Tor and I will stay here to keep an eye on the continent and try to come up with alternative solutions, in case something goes wrong down by the border."

Taking a deep breath, Rick steeled himself for the challenges that lay ahead.

"*Wark!*" 2-Tor squawked. "Pop Quiz! What river serves as a natural aquatic border between Mexico and the US state of Texas?"

"The Rio Grande!" Evie cheered, tugging on her mother's arm. "Mom, can we leave right now?"

"We better!" Mom said. "I pride myself on Cleanaspot's efficiency. Why not our family's, too?"

IN A CROWDED, DARKENED CLASSROOM IN WINTERPOLE HEADQUARTERS, DIANA FOUGHT TO KEEP her eyelids from collapsing. The daily marathon lectures she endured in the junior-agent training program were so dull, she had already counted every tile on the ceiling (there were 256 of them). She had also named all 256. Her favorite tile was Fred, the faded white one over the boy who sat two desks in front of her. She didn't remember the boy's name, but she remembered Fred, because the tile had a blotchy brown stain of mysterious origin.

Put simply, Diana would have rather been anywhere other than Winterpole Headquarters. She never should have listened to her mother when she'd sweetly suggested, "Why don't you take some time off of school, honey?" It had sounded great at first—skipping a few classes at the International School for Exceptional Students, getting a chance to impress her mother with her commitment to Winterpole's mission, finding a distraction from the recent debacle with Vesuvia—but the reality was that Diana still had to complete most of her regular schoolwork; and the more she learned about her mother's employers, the more she felt just as baffled by their methods as she did by her ex-best friend's.

She tried to force herself to find the lessons interesting, but she just couldn't do it. Even if she did agree with Winterpole's primary objectives to protect the environment and regulate world matters, she could not stand their antiquated methods and ancient technology. Recently Winterpole had turned its focus to hunting down "problem people," an assortment of rule breakers who ignored the bylaws.

Winterpole's internship coordinator and junior-agent instructor, Mister Skole, was leading this morning's lecture. To help with his presentation, he enlisted the aid of a slide projector so ancient that it belonged in a museum, or perhaps a mummy's tomb.

"The man you see before you is one of Winterpole's most annoying adversaries," Mister Skole explained, his face bathed in the pale-blue light of the projector. "George Lane and his delinquent family frequently trespass on protected habitats and bird-nap endangered species. Most recently, they circumvented our statutes by creating their own continent right under our noses! He is the very worst. Next slide." He said *next slide*, but there was no one to insert a new slide for him; he was operating the projector by himself.

As the teacher fumbled with the old machine, Diana wondered if the Lanes had taken the time to savor their victory over Winterpole and Vesuvia. Although Diana was glad her ex-best friend hadn't turned the Great Pacific Garbage Patch into New Miami, it didn't feel good to be on the losing team. Come to think of it, that was probably why Mister Snow was so determined to arrest George Lane now.

"Pay attention, class," Mister Skole said, having finally settled the next slide into the projector. "This is Professor Nathaniel Doran, a vegetable smuggler who has been running an illegal botanical refuge in Texas for the past ten years." A man in his early forties appeared on the screen, reclining on a large pile of loose broccoli. His warm eyes and cool smile made Diana think that he was either the most confident man on earth, or he *really* liked broccoli.

"Alas, Winterpole has failed to locate his latest operation despite our best efforts. Maybe one of you kids will spearhead the mission to find Professor Doran and put a stop to his carrot corral!"

None of these problem people appeared to have done anything particularly bad, which made the whole lecture seem irrelevant and unworthy of Diana's attention. She wondered if it was possible to fall asleep with her eyes open. Maybe she was sleeping right now, and she just didn't know it. Her eyelids lowered slowly.

Mister Skole slapped his finger against the projection of the next photo, making Diana jump. The slide that followed was an impressive landscape of the African veld. A woman stood center frame, leaning against a crossbow the size of a bazooka. She was draped in multi-colored animal hides, which did little to conceal the sculpted muscles of her Amazonian figure. A dead zebra lay at her feet, its white stripes brown with dirt. Some of the junior agents gasped audibly. This was the first "problem person" who looked like she deserved to be locked away by Winterpole. Mister Skole dubbed her the Big Game Huntress.

Before Diana could really take in the image, Mister Skole aggressively changed slides. "Next! Those pathetic polluters the Condo Corporation!" Diana's stomach dropped. She knew what was coming. Sure enough, her teacher gestured toward a very unflattering photo of Vesuvia. "We may have apprehended the minuscule mastermind of that rotten bunch, but the threat is far from over." Now Diana was firmly awake. She felt the eyes of her classmates on her. Everyone knew about her friendship with Vesuvia.

It was impossible for Diana to be both her mother's spy among the junior agents *and* a traitor in cahoots with the enemy, but somehow her classmates still treated her like she was both.

The harsh glares of her classmates made it hard for Diana to follow the rest of Mister Skole's presentation. The problem people started to blur together.

"Now, students"—Mister Skole turned to face the class—"who can tell me which of these individuals is the biggest threat to Winterpole? Diana Maple?"

Diana looked up from her notes. "The biggest threat? Um . . . hmm . . . irrelevance?"

Judging by Mister Skole's expression, he wasn't amused

by Diana's attempt to lighten the situation. The boy at the desk next to Diana snapped his hand in the air. Mister Skole smiled in relief. "Yes, Benjamin?"

Benjamin Nagg was one of Diana's fellow junior agent trainees. He had chilling blue eyes that fit right in at Winterpole, and slick black hair that formed a shiny helmet around his overly large head. He was so skinny and pale he almost looked sickly, but when he spoke, he sounded commanding and self-important.

"The biggest threat to Winterpole is George Lane and his children, Mister Skole."

Diana's teacher beamed at Benjamin. "Very good, Mister Nagg."

The boy did not let up. "Anyone who would flaunt his disregard for Winterpole statutes as gratuitously as that man must be stopped. It is outrageous that he and his family would exploit loopholes the way they have. We should make an example of the Lanes, as we did the CEO of the Condo Corporation." Benjamin cast a sidelong glance at Diana when he said that last bit. Diana scowled.

"Eloquently put, Benjamin." Mister Skole's smile grew even wider.

Benjamin nodded. "Not everyone can be the boss's child, Mister Skole, but that doesn't mean we can't all know a thing or two . . . thousand."

Diana nearly growled. She didn't ask to be the daughter of the Secretary of Enforcement. She hated it! Why did Benjamin have it out for her?

Dejected and annoyed, Diana stared out the classroom window into the hallway beyond. Suddenly, Mister Snow walked past the classroom with a retinue of armored enforcement agents—her mother's people. Diana realized that these must be the agents the Director had dispatched to apprehend George Lane from his formerly un-legislate-able home on the eighth continent.

No one would ever describe Diana Maple as an impulsive girl. That personality trait had stuck to Vesuvia like a cherry lollipop to a car seat. But she was tired of her classmates' taunts, she was tired of Benjamin Nagg, and most of all, she was tired of the suspicious looks her mother had been giving her ever since Vesuvia had been exposed as an enemy of Winterpole. So for this one moment, Diana imitated her ex-best friend.

She waited until Mister Skole wasn't looking and then snuck out of the classroom.

Long-distance missions launched from a docking bay on the top floor of Winterpole Headquarters, where an enormous skylight opened so hoverships could depart. Normally the docking bay was empty, save the hulks of neglected hoverships that took up space in a circle around the bay, and the occasional cleaning robots that flitted around like insects, slurping up spills.

But today the bay was a mad house.

Long lines of paperwork experts snaked across the metal floor. Each employee had been assigned a different stack of permission slips to be filled out in anticipation of the mission. Enforcement agents in iceberg-shaped helmets hurried about, armed to the molars with glue guns and other weaponry.

Diana couldn't help but feel a little sorry for Rick and Evie. The full force of Winterpole's might was about to hit them hard. But at least after that nasty business was over, Winterpole would save Australia. Now *that* was something she hoped she'd be there to see. And she would be, if the plan she had set in motion worked.

Diana had decided that to prove to her mother, Mister Skole, Benjamin, and all the rest that she could be just as good as a Winterpole agent as any of them, she would have to work with the best. And who was the best? Mister Snow.

Diana watched as he stood at the center of the docking bay, barking orders. "I want seventeen fully equipped enforcers on every hovership. Have your EMP grenades checked. I will not tolerate any errors, ladies and gentlemen. So do not slip. Do not waver. It is imperative we do not disappoint the Director. His favor is all that matters to us—the humble guardians of the planet Earth. We are going to find George Lane and stop him permanently."

Diana felt a little queasy. Sure, she'd chosen to force her way into the mission for personal reasons, but still, she didn't like the way Mister Snow talked about what they were up to. Winterpole was supposed to legislate the eighth continent, but all anyone was talking about was arresting George Lane and pleasing the Director, not saving Australia. This was bigger than the quirky inventor. Couldn't Winterpole see that?

"Where are those geolocation reports?" Mister Snow shouted over the racket. "Will someone PLEASE get me the geolocation reports?!"

Diana searched the crowded docking bay. She found the missing reports in a stack of cardboard boxes on a dolly. They were hiding behind an artillery tank that looked like an old-fashioned clothing iron strapped with machine guns.

Diana dragged the dolly to the middle of the room where Mister Snow paced impatiently.

"Junior Agent Maple, what are you doing?"

"Here are those—uff!—geolocation reports you requested, sir. I found them over there."

Mister Snow nodded approvingly. "Not bad, Maple. We may make an agent out of you, yet."

"Thank you, sir." Diana smiled proudly. "To that end, I wish to make a request."

"Now is hardly the time, Maple. Can't you see I'm busy?"

Vesuvia had dismissed her the same way many times (albeit with much more colorful language). At any other moment Diana would have given up, but not today. "Sir, I want to go on the mission to the eighth continent."

"Don't be outrageous! This is the most important

operation that Winterpole has ever run. I can't have some trainee getting in the way."

She had expected him to say that. That's why she'd come prepared.

From the pocket of her uniform, Diana withdrew a rolled up piece of cyber paper—the latest advancement in Winterpole paperwork. The synthetic document was made of a durable polymer instead of pulped trees, which made it un-rip-able, un-spill-juice-on-able, and filled with electronic metadata.

Diana pointed the rolled up cyber paper at Mister Snow like it was a fencer's foil. "I need to go on this mission, Mister Snow. To that end, I have acquired a perMission slip, which authorizes me to join you on the eighth continent."

Mister Snow blinked in disbelief. "A perMission slip? Where did you get that?"

The truth was that she had stolen the perMission slip and forged her mother's signature after sneaking out of her classroom. But she wasn't going to tell Mister Snow that.

"Mister Snow, I'm positively shocked that you would ask me that question. Aren't you forgetting Winterpole Statute Twenty-three-dash-fourteen-alpha-eight-with-feet?"

"Eight-with-feet? You mean 'ampersand'?"

"Precisely, Mister Snow. It states that no one may question someone carrying a signed perMission slip without permission."

Lines of sweat streaked from Mister Snow's white sideburns down his cheeks. Diana imagined that this must have been an unusual experience for him. People rarely questioned his vast knowledge of Winterpole statutes, let alone junior agents.

"Very well, Junior Agent Maple." Mister Snow cleared his throat. "You may accompany us. Here, be of use and carry my briefcase."

He tossed the briefcase to her. The leather brick was so heavy it nearly dropped her to her knees. Straining to carry it, Diana couldn't help but smile. *Take that, Benjamin,* she thought smugly. She may have been the "boss's stupid daughter," but theft and forgery were two skills Vesuvia had insisted Diana learn long ago. Sure, they were heinous crimes, but as her ex-best friend had frequently reminded her, they'd only get her in trouble if she got caught.

"MOM, CAN I FLY THE *ROOST?*"
"NO, EVIE, YOU CAN'T FLY THE *ROOST.*"

"But M-o-o-o-o-o-o-o-o-m!"

The trip had gone smoothly so far except for this current fight between Evie and her mother. They were a little more than halfway to Texas, and Rick sat in a cushioned seat at the back of the *Roost*'s bridge, listening to his mother and sister argue. He was trying to study Professor Doran's research in the hope of identifying plants that might help them root the eighth continent, but he was finding it hard to concentrate.

"Hey, Mom," he called out, hoping to distract her from Evie's pleas, "how do you and Dad know Professor Doran?"

His mother almost laughed. "Nathaniel was pursuing his doctorate while your father and I were undergraduates."

"I'm surprised you haven't stayed in better touch," Rick mused. "The more research I conduct, the more it seems like Professor Doran is a fascinating individual."

"Research?" Evie repeated.

"Why yes, just a little."

"How much is 'a little'?"

Rick pulled up a document on his pocket tablet. "I compiled a twelve-page brief on the subject. Feel free to review it."

Grimacing, she took the tablet. "I guess I am curious why we've never met him."

"Well, it wasn't as easy to stay in touch back then," their mother explained. "And you can't stay close to everyone. Still, I hope he can help us."

Evie spun around in her cushioned swivel chair. "I'm going to ask Professor Doran to transform Evie World into a big old jungle where every tree is bigger than the *Roost* and has vines you can swing from and leaves the size of your head! And we can run around and hunt and play, and I'll be like a lioness, queen of the jungle!"

Rick blinked in disbelief. "Lions live on the savannah, not in jungles. And what in Turing's name is *Evie World*?"

Evie snorted, as if the answer to this question was as obvious as the forty-seventh digit of pi. "*Psssh.* Why, it's what we're naming the eighth continent, silly!"

"First of all, there is no way we are naming the eighth continent 'Evie World.' You might as well call it 'Evie Thinks She's the Best Person Ever so We're Naming the Continent After Her Even Though a Lot of Other Important People Helped Make the Eighth Continent Too . . . World.'"

Scratching her chin, Evie mused, "That's not a bad name, actually."

"Forget it, Evie. And second, you can't make the continent

a dense jungle. That would be totally counterproductive to our goal to develop an urban infrastructure capable of sustaining a large permanent population."

Evie clutched her head. "Ugh, Rick. That's so boring you're making my brain hurt. We finally have a vast untapped continent, and your instinct is to make it just like all the others."

"There is way more to my ideas than that."

A noisy beep from Mom's communicator interrupted their argument. She pushed a button on the command console and a pixelated image of Mom's assistant, Catherine, appeared over the windshield.

"Hello, Catherine, what is it?"

Mom's assistant was a pretty and bookish young woman with thick green-rimmed glasses. Two fountain pens kept her wavy red hair tucked behind her ears. "I'm sorry to bother you, Mrs. Lane, but something has come up that requires your immediate attention. I'm sending the video data to you now."

The image shifted from Catherine's face to a wide aerial shot of the ocean. The clear blue water was marred by a huge blob. At first Rick thought it was an island.

"What am I looking at, Catherine?" Mom was all business.

Catherine explained, "Several hours ago, we discovered a massive stain in the South Pacific. Early reconnaissance indicates that it's ink, ma'am."

"Ink?"

"Yes, ma'am. An ink stain. We've been getting reports of seabirds so dirty they can't fly. I don't have numbers yet, but fish are dying, ma'am. Thousands of them. Cleanaspot has received several requests that we intervene."

"Those poor fish," Mom said.

"There's something else. The stain appears to be expanding at an alarming rate. If the current rate of growth continues, it could cover the whole ocean in less than a week."

Mom rose from her chair. "We have to do something right away."

"But Mom!" Evie tugged on her sleeve. "Our mission!"

"Yes, yes, honey. Hold on." Mom downloaded all the info about the stain to her phone. "Catherine, initiate Clean Up Protocol One. Get Charles and Doctor Wong on the phone. Tell them to begin work on a containment procedure. I'll be in touch soon. Don't worry. We'll put a stop to this stain."

"Thank you, Mrs. Lane. I knew you'd know what to do."

The feed switched off, and the windshield returned to the *Roost*'s view of the ocean, sky, and approaching California coastline.

Mom was once again all business. "Rick, Evie, I'm sorry, but I'm going to have to put our trip to Texas on hold."

"But . . . but . . ." Evie muttered in disbelief. "Our new home is in danger. And what about Australia?"

Rick adjusted his glasses. "Evie's right, Mom. This is a crisis."

"A giant stain on the ocean is also a crisis. Didn't you hear what Catherine said? The *whole ocean* could be in danger.

Imagine the ecosystems that could be wiped out. Rick, you know the risks if I do nothing. It'd be a global catastrophe. Cleanaspot has to help." Mom bit her lip and stared out the window, obviously trying to come up with a plan.

Evie looked up from her seat hopefully. "What if 2-Tor met up with us?"

"That's not a bad idea." Rick raced over to the communicator before Mom could argue. He punched in the number for Dad. It started ringing. Once Dad picked up, they could ask him to send 2-Tor to their current location, and when their feathered guardian arrived, they would be back on their way to Professor Doran.

But Dad didn't pick up. That was odd. Odder than the usual Dad oddness, which was quite odd.

Rick tried calling three more times, but there was still no reply.

"Why isn't Dad answering?" Evie asked, worry filling her voice.

Mom patted Evie's head soothingly. "I'm sure he's just working on some experiment with 2-Tor. It's nothing to worry about. But I can't leave the two of you unsupervised. And if we can't get 2-Tor to watch you both . . ." She looked toward the command console.

"No, Mom," Evie pleaded. "Not that, anything but that."

"I'm sorry, Evie," Mom said, sitting back down at the controls.

Rick watched his mother disable the autopilot and enter new coordinates. His heart sank. "Geneva?"

"That's right." Mom looked tough, focused, and all business. "The oceans are in danger, and it's my duty to clean up that stain. I'm sorry that all of these terrible things are happening at once, but we don't have time to take you back to your father on the eighth continent. And it's too dangerous for you to go on a mission alone without me or 2-Tor, so there's only one option: I'm taking you to school."

Evie groaned.

Rick tugged on his mother's arm. "Mom, if we don't go meet Professor Doran now, what will happen to Australia and the eighth continent?"

She rubbed his back soothingly. "Don't get discouraged, honey. We aren't giving up yet. Let me keep trying to reach your father while I evaluate this stain situation, and then I'll reconnect with you later tonight. Meanwhile, do what you can to keep the mission going after you arrive at the International School for Exceptional Students. Research more ways to root the continent. Do a cross-analysis of all the goos, glues, and gruels we may be able to use as waterproof adhesives."

"I'll get right on it, Mom." Rick didn't like this at all, but maybe he'd be able to use the time at school to find an even better way to stop the continent from moving.

Evie tried once more to make her mother reconsider. "Mom, please, I'm begging you, in the name of all that is scientific and awesome, please, PLEASE, don't make us go to school."

Mom was hearing none of it. She filled one of the *Roost*'s

acorn-shaped escape pods with her luggage and other business papers, kissed her children goodbye, and was off to clean up the stain.

When the acorn had flown out of sight, Evie sprinted back to the bridge. Rick chased after her. He opened the bridge doors to find his sister aggressively punching new coordinates into the navigator.

Oh no. Rick had a bad feeling about this. "Evie, what are you doing?"

She glanced over her shoulder at him and grinned. "I'm, uh . . . programming the *Roost* to take a shortcut to school. Well, more of a long cut. You see, I put us back on our original course to Texas."

Rick had no interest in getting between Mom and Evie on this. He wanted to do what his mother had ordered, but they urgently needed to root the continent. According to his Continent Collision Counter, they had less than thirty-five hours before the big crash.

"But Mom said to go straight to school," he moaned feebly.

"We will go to school," Evie said, ". . . eventually."

A FEW HOURS EARLIER . . .

"Eyes front, agents." Mister Snow's stern command came from the cockpit of the lead hovership. "The Great Pacific Garbage Patch is straight ahead."

Diana's heart was beating as fast as it used to on missions with Vesuvia. She hadn't seen the Great Pacific Garbage Patch since it had been transformed into the eighth continent. There was no telling what kind of traps George Lane would have waiting for them.

Diana had been issued one of Winterpole's iceberg helmets, but it was so big it sank over her shoulders. She removed the helmet and peered out the hovership window at the continent below.

The Eden Compound had done its work. A whole continent had appeared where previously a garbage dump had been. The spongy earth of the continent stretched past the horizon, the greenish-brown plain broken only by the occasional rocky outcropping and a few twisting rivers and streams.

Near the shore Diana could make out a small encampment where campfires and a couple of temporary wooden shelters were laid out. There was also a parked hovership that Diana recognized—the *Condor*, George Lane's personal vessel.

The hovership the Winterpole agents were aboard started to descend. *Guess that's where we're headed*, Diana thought, plunging her head back into the oversized helmet.

"Go, go, go!" Mister Snow ordered as the hoverships landed and the doors slid open. Winterpole soldiers spilled out of the ships like plastic army men from overturned toy chests, piling up on top of each other. Diana carefully followed Mister Snow out of the ship as he stepped over the fallen agents, who looked quite comical in their iceberg helmets and three-piece suits.

Diana took a breath of the salty sea breeze. The wind was quite pronounced, which she supposed made sense. After all, the continent was moving speedily toward Australia. Despite the impending danger, Diana found the air quite pleasant.

George Lane approached, wiping his hands on a grease-stained rag. He wore a sweatband high on his forehead so his poofy auburn hair went straight up like a volcanic eruption. At the inventor's side was the seven-foot-tall crow, 2-Tor.

"Did you forget that Winterpole has no jurisdiction over the eighth continent?" George asked without a trace of fear.

Mister Snow showed his best sneer to his adversary.

"Actually, that's no longer an issue."

"Come again?" George Lane blinked.

"Winterpole may intervene if one landmass threatens another; and, as I'm sure you're aware, this 'continent,' as you like to call it, is currently barreling toward Australia."

"That's one of the kinks I'm working out."

"You call the imminent demise of twenty-three million people 'a kink'? I'm not sure if it was your negligence, incompetence, or propensity for evil, Mister Lane, but you've managed to cause quite a bit of havoc. And so, I'm delighted to inform you that you, George Lane, are under arrest." Mister Snow whipped a thick piece of cyber paper out of his jacket and showed it to George. The text glowed.

"Negative! Negative!" squawked 2-Tor. "You may not take him."

"Ah, but we will!" Mister Snow snapped in response.

"I say, over my feathered body!"

Mister Snow signaled his agents. Diana flinched as two dozen ice cannons opened on 2-Tor simultaneously. When the mist cleared, the formerly robotic crow was barely visible through the thick block of ice that now encased him.

Furious, George snatched the cyber paper from Mister Snow's hand and moved to tear it. He grimaced and strained, hunching over to get leverage, but the cyber paper just stretched and creaked like old leather. It wouldn't rip.

Mister Snow and the other agents laughed at George's frustration. Diana was the only one who didn't.

George threw the cyber paper on the ground in disgust.

"You shouldn't have frozen my bird."

"Ah, yes, get angry." Mister Snow licked his lips with more relish than a jumbo hot dog. "Poor Georgey. No more excuses. No more escape plans. Now, at long last, you are coming with us."

"Didn't we do this once already?"

"Yes, but last time I could only place you under house arrest. This time I have the authority to take you to the Prison at the Pole."

Defiantly, George said, "I'm not afraid of the Prison at the Pole."

Mister Snow snorted. "Give it time to convince you."

The agents laughed uproariously. George Lane looked shattered as they bound his wrists behind his back with a squid-cuff and dragged him onto one of the hoverships.

As Mister Snow watched the agents carry his adversary away, Diana approached. "Mister Snow, I'd like to take a squad and inspect the compound. My guess is that the Lanes were working on a way to stop the continental collision. Maybe we can find their research and use it to help us."

"Don't interrupt me. I'm savoring my victory." Mister Snow smirked and hummed a triumphant ditty.

Diana watched, frozen, as the agents began unloading the supplies to set up their base of operations on the eighth continent. Everything was going right. So why did it all feel so wrong?

THE *ROOST* SWEPT OVER THE TEXAS HILL COUNTRY. RICK AND EVIE PRESSED THEIR NOSES AGAINST A window, watching from their perch on the bridge as cedar forests and herds of longhorn cattle scrolled past.

"It's so green," Evie remarked in surprise. "And look at the cute cities! I always thought Texas would be brown and desolate, like something out of an old western movie."

"Nonsense," Rick said, admiring the scenery. "If Texas was its own country, it would have the fourteenth largest economy in the world. It has almost twice the gross domestic product of Switzerland."

"What's so gross about Switzerland's domestic product?"

Rick sighed. "Sometimes I wonder if you ask such silly questions on purpose. Not that kind of gross. It means the total value of everything the country produces; and although Texas is just a state, it produces a lot. Did you know that back a couple hundred years ago, Texas *was* its own country, called The Republic of Texas? They had a President and everything."

"Heh!" Evie snorted. "You sound like 2-Tor. Is it time for a quiz?"

Rick tried to smile. "You wanna know the honest truth? I miss 2-Tor. Even with all our wild adventures, we've never been totally on our own before, without the supervision of 2-Tor or Mom or Dad. It doesn't feel safe."

"I know!" Evie chirped. "Isn't it great?"

Before Rick could answer, music started playing from the command console, indicating that they were coming up on their destination.

Ahead they could see the snaking water of the Rio Grande, the river that divided the southern border of the United States from its neighbor Mexico. At a bend in the river, a patchwork of multicolored squares stretched northward like a quilt: farmland. From this distance, Evie couldn't identify the various crops, but the sheer diversity of them astounded her, especially in this environment. Sure, Texas wasn't a desert like she had expected, but still! They must have been using some seriously high-tech watering cans to get such plants to grow here.

Rick aimed the *Roost* at a small compound of portable buildings on the eastern side of the farm. Together, he and Evie braced themselves as their hovership landed on its shock-absorbent roots in front of the compound's gated entrance. Their stomachs flipped as the bridge realigned with the ship's new orientation.

Evie and Rick emerged from the *Roost* and were struck by the midday heat. Evie took off her blue hoodie and tied it around her waist, then rolled up her gray pants above her skinny knees. A Geneva Genomes baseball cap kept the sun out of her eyes. Rick's hair was damp with sweat, and although he had rolled up the sleeves of his button-down shirt, the under-parts of his elbows were soaked with perspiration.

"Ugh!" Evie squinted in the bright sunlight. "It's like getting hit in the face with a hair dryer."

"This heat is oppressive, but we gotta keep going."

Beyond the fence, worker robots carried heavy loads of fertilizer, seeds, and farming equipment across the compound. The robots were orange, but their color wasn't the strangest thing about them.

"They look like carrots," said Evie.

"Yeah," Rick replied. "Eight-foot-tall carrots."

Evie was about to call out to the robo-carrots and ask them to open the gate, when she heard some rustling of plants in the cornfield to her right. She exchanged a glance with her brother. "Did you hear that?" she whispered.

"It sounded like—" Rick paused.

This time Evie could clearly make out the sound of a person grunting. "There's definitely someone there," she said. She pulled apart the thick green cornstalks and entered the field before her brother could tell her to stop.

They followed the sound through the dense thicket, emerging after a short walk in a clearing. A boy about Rick's age stood in the middle of the circle. He wore leather chaps over his denim jeans, and a frilled shirt adorned with a bolo tie. The gold slide on the tie was shaped like a chili pepper. A thick fibrous belt hung low on his hips, and a scabbard dangled from it. Fitted in the scabbard was an old machete, a kind of macho knife. A wide-brimmed cowboy hat ten sizes too big was perched atop the boy's head. He had dark copper-colored skin and keen eyes, and beside him there was a pile of corn half as tall as he was.

Evie and Rick watched silently as the boy raised a lasso above his head, swinging it in a circle a few times before grunting loudly and flinging the ring of rope. He snagged a cornstalk and pulled the lasso tight, stripping the ears of corn off the plant. The corn landed in the pile beside him, and with a proud look of accomplishment, the boy recoiled his lasso.

"Wow!" Evie exclaimed, unable to stop herself from applauding. "That was amazing!"

The boy leaped into the air and spun around, startled. "Screaming scorpions! Where did y'all come from?"

Rick held up his hands defensively. "Don't shoot! Or, don't lasso, or whatever."

"We're trying to find Professor Doran," Evie said. "It's important."

The boy's eyes darted between the siblings. "I don't reckon the Prof's expecting visitors. Who's we, exactly?"

"Professor Doran is an old friend of our parents," Evie explained. "My name is Evie Lane, and this is my brother, Rick. Our business with the professor is really urgent." She glanced in the direction of the compound.

The boy tipped back his hat and wiped his brow with a

handkerchief. "The Prof is conducting a mighty important experiment right now. He'd be madder than a mango in mustard if I interrupted."

Evie whispered to Rick. "Do something! We have to talk to Professor Doran right now."

Rick whispered back, "What can I do? If we make him mad he might not help us."

The boy folded his arms over his puffed out chest. "While y'all're whispering like a Fort Worth wind, I can hear y'all clear as cooked onion."

Rick's cheeks turned the color of his hair. "Sorry. It's just that we're here on an important mission for our parents."

"Your parents?" The boy's eyes lit up like the headlights of a pickup truck. "Wait a gosh darn minute. Did y'all say your name was Lane? As in, Lane Industries?"

"That's right," Evie said. "What's it to ya?"

"Well, shoot, ma'am. Lane Industries. Hoverships! Robo-intelligence. Without your family, I wouldn't have my carrying carrots, my hover horse, or all sorts a things."

"That's Lane Industries," Rick said with a proud smile.

"Well, by rhubarb I oughtta take y'all to the Prof right away. Just let me finish up my chores."

Grabbing his lasso, the boy whirled like a tornado. He threw out the rope and reeled it back with a snap. Each pull brought in a wheelbarrow's worth of corn.

The boy called over his shoulder. "When I do it like this, it always makes me feel like I'm playing *Lasso Lunatic* on my Game Zinger."

Rick gasped like he'd uncovered buried treasure. "You've played *Lasso Lunatic*? That's, like, one of the rarest video games of all time!"

"Play it? Hooo-eee! I got a copy signed by the whole development team. I'll let you borrow it if you want."

Rick's mouth hung open. Evie waved a hand in front of his face to make sure he hadn't slipped into a video-game-induced coma.

The boy with the lasso finished roping corn and started walking toward the compound.

"What about the corn?" Rick asked, indicating the huge pile of yellow ears in the middle of the clearing.

"Aw, the carrying carrots will pick that up when they come through these parts. So follow me! Don't want this opportunity to go bad on the vine."

"Hey wait a minute," Evie said as they started to follow. "You never told us your name, Mister Cowboy."

"The name's Sprout Sanchez, ma'am." He flashed a ten-gallon grin. "Now follow me. We've gotta get y'all to the Prof right away."

8

RICK, EVIE, AND THEIR NEW GUIDE SPROUT CUT A QUICK PATH THROUGH THE COMPOUND. RICK tried not to get distracted by the incredible sights. Professor Doran's farm was the coolest science lab Rick had ever seen. It felt so . . . organic. And not like overpriced-fruit-at-the-grocery-store organic. There was something about the way the crops and the buildings all fit together. Everything felt natural, like all the pieces were in their proper place, which was funny because the space felt messy too. It was all just . . . right.

When he asked Sprout about this, the boy kicked a pebble down the dirt path. "Well, shoot, Rick, that's just the Prof's way of working. He lets everything grow the way it wants—even me. The Prof says that's why I grew so wild, because no one tended to me."

"You don't have any parents?" Evie looked concerned.

"No, ma'am. Just the Prof, and the robots on the farm. But they're more like pets than parents, if y'all know what I mean."

Rick couldn't imagine what life would be like without any parents. He depended on his mom and dad for everything. His mom encouraged him and praised him, and his father challenged him and piqued his curiosity.

Rick took a closer look at Sprout—at the way he stood straight as a celery stalk and rarely let that big smile leave his face. Only recently had Rick found out that his dad had been an orphan himself. It was something Doctor Grant had told him in the Arctic, back on the Mastercorp research submarine. Rick had no idea who his biological grandfather was, but he knew his dad had been lucky to have Jonas Lane adopt him. It appeared that Sprout had been lucky too, having found his own brilliant scientist to mentor and care for him. It made sense that Professor Doran would be friends with Rick's parents.

Sprout pointed over the ridge in front of them. "The Prof's lab is just past here. Try not to look if you can help it."

The kids crested the ridge and beheld a startling sight. The beautiful patchwork of farmland ended abruptly, at the edge of a barren waste. Beyond the ridge, the land was dark and cracked, the terrain pockmarked with huge craters. Every few moments, a smoking light would cut through the sky and smash the ground with a loud explosion.

KRA-BOOM!

Rick covered his ears. "What are they doing?"

"Bomb testing," Sprout muttered. "Sometimes missiles. Sometimes firearms. Some days they send armies of robots out there to pummel each other."

The vein in Rick's forehead throbbed in anger and disgust. What a terrible contradiction, this vast absence of life so close to all that Professor Doran had created.

"Who is 'they'?" Rick asked finally, his craving for justice bubbling in his throat.

"Weapons manufacturer. Goes by the name of Mastercorp."

Rick knew Mastercorp all too well. They were the corporation that had originally funded his father's development of the Eden Compound. When his dad discovered that Mastercorp wanted to use the Eden Compound as a weapon, he gave up on his trash-conversion research for years. It wasn't until Rick and Evie discovered what their father had been up to so long ago that he finally allowed the compound to be used. And even then he'd warned them to be careful about attracting Mastercorp's attention.

Everything Rick had seen of Mastercorp freaked him out. The corporation was dangerous. It had pressured his father. It had imprisoned his dad's thesis advisor, Doctor Grant. It had chewed up the earth here in Texas and countless other places. What a waste. The farther he could keep his family from Mastercorp, the better.

Sprout hocked a big loogie off the ridge, interrupting Rick's thoughts. Rick watched the spit descend until it spattered on the dirt below. Sprout tipped his hat to Evie. "Sorry, ma'am. That was mighty inconsiderate of me. I just can't abide them Mastercorp folk. It makes me right angry."

Evie stared at Sprout for a moment, letting a wry smile

creep up on her face. Then she turned and spat. The slick glob of spit was the size of a Ping-Pong ball, and it soared over the ridge in a smooth arc.

"Yuck." Rick scrunched up his nose.

"Hee hee hoo!" Sprout slapped his thighs excitedly. "That's my kind of spitting, ma'am."

Evie wiped her mouth with the back of her hand, blushing. "You can call me Evie, Sprout. 'Ma'am' makes me sound like an old lady."

Sprout nodded. He stepped aside to make room for Rick at the edge of the ridge. "C'mon, Rick. Give it a try."

Rick thought spitting was gross and undignified, but if Sprout thought that it was cool, he didn't want to disappoint the young cowboy. After all, it was rare that kids his age invited him to do anything at all.

Rick shuffled between Evie and Sprout, staring at the shrapnel and missile silos in the distance. Summoning all his anger and frustration—at the devastation Mastercorp had wrought upon the earth, at the rules Winterpole had used to torment his family for so long, at Vesuvia and her nasty pink robots—Rick summoned a huge loogie and spat.

"Agh! Gross!" Evie squealed. Spitting, apparently, wasn't one of Rick's strong suits. A little white froth dribbled out of his mouth and onto his chin.

"Ha ha hee hoo hoo!" Sprout slapped his thighs again. "That's showing them, Rick!"

"This is a big waste of time," Rick roared. "We have to get back to the mission. The eighth continent is in danger!"

He stomped away, looking for Professor Doran's lab.

Evie chased after him. "Aw, Rick! Come back. We didn't mean it."

Sprout caught up and guided them to the largest building on the site, a three-story barn made of sheet metal. The top floor was a greenhouse, encased in glass, where Rick imagined Professor Doran conducted his coolest botanical experiments.

"Mind where y'all step," Sprout cautioned, pushing open the barn's sliding doors. "It's a jungle in here."

He meant it literally. Rick and Evie followed him into the barn, eyes wide in amazement. Prehistoric-looking vines and plants hung from a leafy canopy that covered the ceiling. Butterflies fluttered from flower to flower.

"Uh, how are we supposed to get through?" Rick asked.

"Follow me!" Sprout replied. He drew his old machete from its scabbard and hacked away at the vines.

Evie grinned. "Cool! Can I try?"

Sprout handed her the sword. "Sure, go ahead."

Evie chopped the plants with gusto, cutting a path through the barn jungle. Rick winced. "Aren't these Professor Doran's plants?"

"Oh sure," Sprout said, tipping back his hat. "The Prof uses his super fertilizer on everything in the barn, so it doesn't matter if you chop things down. It all just grows back. He thinks it's funny. See?" Sprout pointed back the way they had come. The entrance to the barn was hidden by the vines they had slashed a minute earlier.

"Incredible!" Rick exclaimed.

Sprout clapped Rick heartily on the back. "Well, shoot! I reckoned someone as smart as you would appreciate the Prof's genius."

Rick smiled. He had only known Sprout an hour, but he already cared very much about what the boy thought of him. Rick would not have been able to explain it if someone asked him, but he didn't think he had ever met someone as nice or as cool as Sprout Sanchez.

Grunting with exertion, Evie continued to hack away at the plants in front of her. "These vines are growing back almost as fast as I can cut through them!"

Sprout laughed. "The Prof says if you ain't willing to put in the effort to talk to him, then whatever you had to say wasn't important enough. Here, let me." He took the machete from Evie and started swinging wildly at the plants, chopping his way to the far side of the barn. Rick and Evie joined him at the wall, where a staircase of yellow dandelions as wide as Hula-Hoops led to the upper floors of the barn.

Minding where they stepped, the kids followed Sprout up the organic stairs. As they reached the ceiling on the second floor, Rick saw that a five-foot hole had been cut out to accommodate the dandelion staircase. The kids climbed through the opening, emerging into bright sunlight.

From the outside, this floor had looked like a greenhouse—given the way that it was covered with glass—but strangely, there were no plants here, just big gray machines with tanks and conveyor belts, chugging away.

At the far end of the room, a man stood at a worktable with his back to the children. His long white lab coat flowed about his ankles. He swirled a large beaker of colorful chemicals, then added the solution to a metal vat in front of him.

"Hey, Prof!" Sprout called out. "Look at what I got here! Visitors!"

Professor Nathaniel Doran turned to face the newcomers. Under his lab coat he wore dress slacks and a polka-dotted sweater. A surgical mask covered his mouth, its white color contrasting against his rich dark skin and close-cut black hair. He pulled off the mask and scrutinized the children with wise, cautious eyes. "Yes? And who might you—" the professor stopped as he studied Evie's face.

She raised an eyebrow at his gaze. "What?"

"You're . . . You're Melinda Washer's daughter."

"Who?" Evie asked.

"Your mother is—sorry. When I knew her, she wasn't married. Melinda Lane. You're George and Melinda's children." He pointed a finger at Rick. "I see him in you, son."

Rick felt his cheeks grow warm. Maybe getting Professor Doran's help rooting the continent would be easier than Rick thought. "That's right, sir. We're Rick and Evelyn—Evie—Lane. Our dad sent us here to meet with you. Our mom was going to join us, but things came up."

"That is unfortunate." Professor Doran bowed his head. "I'm sorry to hear that. I have not had old friends visit in quite some time. Did Sanchez show you around?"

"Sure did, Prof!" Sprout said. "They're smart, tough, everything you like, sir."

Professor Doran nodded. "I'd expect nothing less from the children of a scientist as brilliant and strong as Melinda Washer."

Rick stepped forward. "Professor, we have urgent business to discuss with you."

"Ah, yes," the professor said. "I don't suppose you would have come all this way for a social call. Let's step into my office. If your parents sent you to me, I'd imagine that there can only be one reason."

"Is that right?" Sprout looked at Rick and Evie with new eyes. "What's the reason?"

Professor Doran raised an eyebrow. "Why, isn't it obvious? The whole world is in danger."

A WIND KICKED UP, BLOWING DUST AND A FEW LOOSE SEEDS THROUGH THE WARM AIR. EVIE covered her face to shield her eyes, but the carrying carrots didn't mind the breeze. They continued to proceed, single file, into the *Roost*, dragging large canvas sacks beside them.

It was hard to believe that she and Rick had arrived in Texas a few hours ago. So much had happened. Professor Doran had taken them into his office, a quiet wooden study in which potted plants occupied every available surface. He had listened carefully to their story, which they started from the very beginning, with Dad's Winterpole troubles and the need to create a place where their family could be free. When they finished the tale, getting to the part where the meteor of pink robo-animals crashed into the eighth continent and knocked it onto its collision course with Australia, Professor Doran leaned back in his chair and stared at the ceiling for a long time. "I see. That is quite a predicament you have found yourselves in."

"Yes, that's why you must help us!" Rick insisted. "Our father said you're the only one who can."

"Your father? Hmm . . . I wonder." The professor's expression grew distant.

"What's wrong?" Evie asked, confused by the strange shift in his tone of voice.

"Nothing," Professor Doran said. "The Amazonian Super Root is what you need. Come with me; we'll have to check in storage."

He led the children across the compound to what looked like a storm cellar sticking out of the ground. The cellar concealed a deep subterranean cavern, where boxes were stacked floor to ceiling as far as the eye could see. Evie danced as they piled into a little motorcar. She was so excited Professor Doran was helping them.

The professor drove through the maze of stacks and parked abruptly in front of a wooden crate that was painted bright green. "All right, here we are," he said as he pried open the lid of the green box so the others could look inside. At the bottom of the box was a bit of hay used for packing cushion, and in the center, a smaller green box.

Evie reached for it. "Is that—"

"The Amazonian Super Root," Sprout affirmed. Professor Doran opened the small box and took out a black bulb the size of a head of garlic. "It's a plant with mighty fine cellular properties. It grows faster than weeds, and the Prof's fertilizers can accelerate that growth. The root's stronger than a bull and thicker than an elephant's butt!"

Evie snorted at that, receiving a nudge from Rick in return. But if Sprout thought it was funny, then Evie was going to laugh. Each of his jokes was more hilarious than the last.

"This should be enough to solve your runaway continent problems," Professor Doran explained. "But why should we stop there?" He tossed the bulb back into the box and snapped the lid shut. "You have a whole continent to build—a blank slate where you can create anything your imagination can dream up. You shouldn't settle for an empty canvas. You need forests and jungles, fields of wildflowers, every biome on earth, and perhaps more! Your mother would appreciate such a beautiful landscape. I'm sure you will too. So please, let me give you the seeds you need to create this world."

Evie could not agree to this plan fast enough. It made her vast continent of jungle adventure appear even more clearly in her mind. Rick, meanwhile, expressed concern about vegetation densities and anticipated population numbers. Ultimately, however, he agreed that passing up this opportunity would be ill-advised—though he urged them all to compile the seeds and saplings as quickly as possible, as there would be no continent left to plant flora on if it crashed into Australia.

"You have quite a lot of work ahead of you, Evelyn," Professor Doran observed as Sprout and Rick worked with the carrying carrots to swiftly gather the supplies.

Evie shrugged. "Having work is fine, as long as you make it fun."

Professor Doran shook his head in amazement. "You're so much like your mother. That sounds like something she would say."

Evie glowered. "I'm nothing like my mother."

"Huh, huh, huh," Professor Doran chuckled. "That's *exactly* what Melinda would say."

When the seeds were all cleaned up, Rick and Sprout ran over to where Evie and Professor Doran were watching.

Sprout nearly jumped out of his cowboy boots. "Prof! Prof! Rick and I just came up with a mighty fine plan."

"Oh?"

"He's a genius, this one." Sprout threw an arm around Rick's neck. Rick grinned, looking happy to be praised. Evie scowled. Sprout was a rough-and-tumble kid, just like her. Why would he think a super nerd like Rick was cool?

"So what's the 'mighty fine plan'?" the professor asked.

"I'm all riled up thinking about what this here super root can do," Sprout explained. "Anchor a whole continent? Hoo-wee! I gotta see it for my own self, Prof. I wanna go with these here good folks and see the eighth continent!"

Evie had to admit, this was the best idea she had heard in a while. They could use the help rooting the eighth continent, and truthfully, she wanted to spend more time with the wild cowboy. She didn't think she'd ever met someone as nice or as cool as Sprout Sanchez.

Professor Doran was, however, slightly less excited about this idea. "That is out of the question, Sanchez. I need you here with me, tending to the crops and the labs. We still have a great deal of work to do—work that will enable us to aid more good folks like the Lanes here."

"Aw, well shoot, Prof. Way to call off the hootenanny." Sprout snapped his fingers in an "aww rats" kind of way and walked off, leaving Rick, Evie, and Professor Doran behind.

The carrying carrots loaded the last crates and sacks on the *Roost*. Professor Doran walked Rick and Evie to their hovership's entry ramp, where he said his goodbye. "Please pass my regards on to Melinda, and your father too. I hope my seeds add beauty to your new world."

"So do we." Evie tried to smile, even though she was sad Sprout would not be joining them.

"And be careful with this." Professor Doran placed the small chest containing the super root in Evie's outstretched hands. "Take good care of it. The Amazonian Super Root is exceptionally rare."

"I will. I promise." Evie untied her hoodie from around her waist and put it back on, then slipped the super root into her pocket.

"Hey wait a minute!" Rick complained. "I'm older. I should be the one to hold the root."

"I've got it," Evie said, hugging the small chest protectively.

"You're always losing things!"

"Am not!"

"Children," Professor Doran cut in. "Surely your time is more valuable than this argument. Get going."

A few minutes later, Professor Doran's botanical lab was behind them, and the *Roost* was over the Pacific Ocean on its way back to the eighth continent, its every compartment filled with Professor Doran's many gifts.

But then a strange noise interrupted their journey.

Thok! Thok!

"Did you hear that?" Rick asked, sounding concerned.

"It's probably the crates of seeds sliding around the storage hold."

"That makes sense," he said. "But you know what, just to be safe . . ." And with that, he initiated autopilot.

Evie tapped the communicator on the command console. "So, umm, you're going to think it's weird that I'm saying this, but I feel like it's time we call Mom."

Rick wiggled a finger in his ear like he thought it was clogged. "Call Mom?! Who are you? What have you done with Evie? Mom will lose her lid when she finds out we didn't go back to school."

"I'm serious, Rick! It's not like she's going to tell us to give the super root back to Professor Doran. And besides, that stain on the ocean is freaking me out. I'm just hoping that maybe Mom has it cleaned up by now, and we can all go root the continent together."

"Good point."

They initiated the call with Mom, but it was Catherine, not her, whose face appeared on the screen. Her eyes were red and puffy and her cheeks were streaked with tears. Evie's stomach curled in on itself.

"Oh, kids! Oh, I'm so sorry!"

Evie's voice trembled. "What is it, Catherine? What's wrong?"

Mom's assistant wiped her eyes on her sleeve. "Your mother arrived just a short while ago. But as soon as she got here, Winterpole showed up, and they arrested her!"

"What?" Rick screamed. "No!"

"One of Cleanaspot's rival corporations, called Ink-A-Spot, has accused us of planting the stain on the ocean, in order to profit from cleaning it up."

"That's outrageous!" Evie said. "What a diabolical blot—er, I mean plot!"

"Winterpole said your mother was being held for creating the stain."

"But that's impossible! She was with us when the stain appeared."

"I know, kids. I'm sorry. We're doing everything we can to get her free. I'm still trying to get in touch with your father, but I haven't been able to reach him. Tell your teachers you can't go home. Whatever you do, *don't* leave your school's campus. It's not safe to be out there on your own. Do you hear me? Stay at school."

"Um . . ." Evie felt a heavy weight on her chest. She missed the simple days when her father was under house arrest and only Winterpole was trying to ruin their lives.

Catherine switched off the communicator and Rick turned to his sister. "We have to get back to the eighth continent right away. We need to find Dad, and hopefully he can give us some simple explanation for why he hasn't picked up anyone's calls. And then he can help us anchor the continent and come up with a way to set Mom free."

"Okay." Evie could not hide the worry in her voice. "Let's do it."

There was another loud thump from behind them. *THOK!* The kids turned.

The sound was coming from inside a crate that had been left on the bridge. "Do you remember what's inside that thing?" Evie asked.

Rick gulped. "I don't even remember leaving the box here."

Evie eyed it suspiciously. By this point, whatever was in the crate had started banging against the wooden sides of the box. Evie took a few steps toward the crate, then noticed that her brother hadn't moved. "Rick, come on!" she whisper-screamed. Evie's heart raced as she popped the lid off the box. "It's a bunch of seeds. And a—"

"And a what?" Rick asked, finally approaching the crate.

"And a . . . cowboy hat?"

Suddenly, the cowboy hat moved. Only it wasn't just a hat. It was a boy. A very familiar one . . .

"Howdy again!" he yelled as he burst from the crate and seeds tumbled off his stocky shoulders.

"Sprout! You came!" Evie cheered.

Rick brushed a few loose seeds off of Sprout's shoulders. "It's so good to see you, but won't Professor Doran be mad you left?"

Evie shoved her brother. "Ugh! Why are you bringing Sprout down? He's here. That's all that matters."

"Aw, Rick, don't worry none about that," said Sprout. "If the Prof wants me to go back, he'll leave a message on my phone."

He clicked his phone on to prove his point. "You have—seventeen—unread messages from—Professor Doran—marked—urgent," said the soothing voice of the phone. Sprout grinned sheepishly and stuck the device back in his back pocket.

"So this is y'all's hovership? Hoo-wee!" Sprout sauntered over to the command console and plopped down in a chair. "These controls are mighty fine. Look at how fast we're going!"

"That's nothing!" Evie grabbed the *Roost*'s controls and increased the throttle. "Check this out!"

The kids felt a pull as the *Roost* accelerated, pushing them back against their seats. Sprout bounced in his chair. "Yee-haw! This is more fun than a radish round-up."

"Evie! That's too fast!" Rick moaned.

"See?" Evie smiled at Sprout. "Rick's always complaining that we're going too fast."

"Am not!" Rick grumbled. He sat in the chair next to their new friend. "Hey, Sprout, we've got some time before we reach the eighth continent. Wanna try this new RPG I got for my Game Zinger?"

Sprout brightened at the sight of the pocket game

player. "I've wanted to play this game for a heckuva long time. It's awful nice of you to let me borrow it."

"My pleasure, Sprout. What are friends for?"

"Hey! Don't leave me out if you're going to play," Evie admonished them. She felt like Rick was using the word *friend* just to taunt her. She had finally met a kid her age who was super cool, and Rick, as usual, was getting in the way. She bristled and cranked up the throttle a little more, pushing the *Roost* and her thoughts forward.

They made good time crossing the ocean, but a few hours later as they neared the eighth continent's last known position, an alert came up on the bridge's monitors.

"What's that awful racket?" Sprout asked, covering his ears.

"Someone's following us." Rick pushed Evie out of the way and grabbed the controls. "Sprout, get to the observation deck. See if you can acquire a visual on whoever's behind us."

"Yes, sir. I'll lasso them instigators. That'll put them right in their place."

"Evie, where's the super root?"

"I've got it," Evie said, touching the small chest in the pocket of her hoodie.

"Leave it with me," Rick said. "It'll be safer."

"I've got it!" Evie insisted. "Sheesh!"

Sick of her brother's nagging, Evie followed Sprout to the back of the *Roost*. They reached the door to the observation deck, breathless.

"Do you think it'll be hard to spot them varmints chasing us?"

"We'll find out soon enough." Evie unlocked the safety latch and opened the door. A dozen pink robo-birds were perched on the guardrail. They chirped and flapped their wings and tilted their heads and whirred their gears. The tiny TV screens in their breasts displayed video of their cursed owner, Vesuvia Piffle. The little blond monster on the screen kept squawking "I hate you! I hate you!" Very articulate.

"How does she keep finding us?" Evie shouted at the birds. "She's supposed to be in prison!"

"Who's she?" asked Sprout, sounding quite confused.

Evie pointed at the mad face on one of the screens. "That crazy pink-obsessed jerk, Vesuvia Piffle."

At that, the birds shrieked and attacked Evie.

Evie flailed wildly. The birds ripped at her arms and legs. One tried to nest in her hair.

"Gah! I hate these things!" She swatted at the birds. Sprout rushed to pull them off.

The fluttering robots pinched Evie by the hood of her sweatshirt and hoisted her into the air. "Evie!" Sprout cried. He reached out to grab her. His fingers brushed against Evie's, but they couldn't get a good grip, and soon Evie was yanked even farther from the *Roost*.

Sprout unhooked his lasso from his belt and took careful aim. "I've got you!" He flung the loop of rope. Evie reached, fighting hard against her captors, and grabbed hold of Sprout's lasso. He began to reel Evie in with an impressive display of strength.

But the birds were not about to give up their prey so easily. Their little mechanical wings flapped wildly, their sharp plastic beaks pecking at Evie until her grip began to slip.

"Don't you dare let go, missy!" Sprout called.

Evie felt something shifting in the pocket of her hoodie. It was the box with the super root. It hung halfway out of her pocket, about to fall. She grabbed it, but the bird pinching her wrist pecked her hand. She recoiled in pain, dropping the box. It tumbled through the open air and shattered upon hitting the crashing waves. The bulb and the broken pieces of box sank beneath the surface.

"Oh no! The super root!" Evie cried out, tears hot on her face. She broke the grip of the pink robo-birds and swung away on Sprout's lasso. The birds must have seen she was going to smash them flat as tin foil. They retreated from the *Roost*, the videos of Vesuvia still shrieking, "I hate you! I hate you!"

Soon the birds had flown out of sight. Evie hung mournfully from the lasso while Sprout pulled her back up to the observation balcony.

Evie threw the end of the lasso to Sprout and stormed back inside of the *Roost*. No part of her wanted to tell her brother what happened, but there was no time to be coy.

She entered the bridge. "Rick . . . Rick!"

"What?" He was focused on the controls.

"I lost the super root."

"Ha ha. Very funny."

"No, um . . . Rick . . ."

He spun around in his seat, and when he saw her face his mouth fell open. Turning back around, Rick pushed the *Roost* into a dive. They nearly smashed into the surface of the ocean, pulling up at the last second to ensure a more delicate landing. They parked on the water where Evie had seen the root go under, but all traces of the root were gone.

They booted up the *Roost*'s deep-water sensors, but as they searched the ocean floor, they received disheartening news. The root had fallen from Evie's pocket over a section of the ocean floor lined with hydrothermal vents called the East Pacific Rise. These vents were fissures—cracks in the earth's crust—through which superheated water escaped. Not a trace of the super root was found. Rick's best guess was that the root bulb fell too close to the boiling water and disintegrated.

At first Rick didn't lecture her for losing the super root. He didn't yell or get mad. But Evie could see that crease in his forehead, and how he gritted his teeth so hard that his jaw pushed out his cheeks. He was furious. He blamed her for losing the root.

Evie blamed herself too. She couldn't believe she had been so clumsy. One second she was holding the root in her hand and the next it was gone. *Those darn robo-birds from Condo Corp.* It didn't matter that their owner was locked up in the Prison at the Pole; Vesuvia Piffle was still making trouble for Rick and Evie.

What a catastrophe. Evie had convinced Rick to break their promise to Mom and gone to Texas without her. Now Mom was in danger. Evie and Rick weren't safe. And no one had heard from Dad. Worst of all, Rick's Continent Collision Counter showed only thirty hours remaining until the eighth continent smashed into Australia. They'd already used up so much time, and they were no closer to achieving their goals. How could they root the continent without a root?

"We should go back to Professor Doran's lab," Rick suggested. "And pick up another super-root bulb."

Sprout sucked air through his teeth. "I'm afraid that won't be possible, Rick. I know for a fact that this here was the only super root the Prof had. We might be able to look for a new one in the jungle where the root grows, but the Amazon is far away and it would take a long while."

Evie punched one of the pilot chairs. "Dang it! So what can we do?"

"Gimme some time to think about it. Maybe I can come up with a plan." Sprout smiled. "Don't worry, Evie. I'll fix this here problem."

They fired up the *Roost*'s engines and continued on to the eighth continent, figuring when they found Dad he would have some ideas. As the continent appeared in their sights, Evie felt some of the tension ease from her neck and shoulders.

"It's nice to be back home," she said. "I could really use some good news for a change."

But as they flew past the Lanes' encampment, they saw that the place was ransacked. Chairs were overturned. Supplies had been dumped all over the ground.

The Lane kids exchanged worried looks. "Now, let's not get all riled up," said Sprout. "Maybe there's a good explanation for everything."

Evie desperately wanted to believe her new friend. She could tell that her brother did as well. He gritted his teeth in determination as he flew the *Roost* over the camp and continued inland, searching for their missing father.

But as they landed the *Roost* on a hilltop overlooking the encampment, Evie's heart sank so deep she felt like it might fall into one of those hydrothermal vents.

Dad and 2-Tor were nowhere to be seen.

SPROUT TIPPED BACK HIS COWBOY HAT AND SCRATCHED HIS BROW. "SO THIS AIN'T HOW YOUR camp is supposed to look, I reckon?"

"Not at all," Rick replied, pacing back and forth across the *Roost*'s bridge. "The encampment should be clean and organized."

"And Dad and 2-Tor should be here, trying to figure out how to solve the continent-collision problem," Evie added.

Rick turned on his heel. "Let's not forget that that particular problem had *already been solved* before someone had to go and drop the super root in the ocean."

"Come on, Rick. That's not fair."

"Fair?! What's not fair is that I warned you. I warned you, Evie. And you mocked me." Rick wanted to throw his sister in the ocean. "All I hope is that when the time comes to build the eighth continent's permanent settlement, you'll trust my judgment."

For once, Evie didn't have a response. Rick could tell that she felt truly horrible about what she'd done. Pangs of guilt began to creep into his chest—he probably shouldn't have yelled at her so intensely. But after all that had happened, was it wrong of him to feel like she just didn't take the whole situation seriously enough? Being in control of the eighth continent was the only way Rick was ever going to fit in anywhere. Evie had no idea how much it meant to him.

"We should at least go outside and look, right y'all?" Sprout suggested in an obvious effort to diffuse the tension. Rick nodded in response; and he, Sprout, and Evie promptly exited the *Roost*.

Their throats tightened as they took stock of the area surrounding the hilltop. To the south lay the abandoned settlement. The embers in the campfire were cold; it was unclear how long the fire had been out. A few of the wooden huts the family had built to live and work in had been smashed. Doors hung off their hinges. There were holes punched in the grassy roofs.

"What's that?" said Evie, motioning east. Rick's stomach dropped as he saw what had attracted Evie's attention.

"That ain't nothing but some buildings," volunteered Sprout.

"Yes, but we haven't constructed any other buildings on the continent," said Rick, his voice hushed.

"Maybe Dad moved his workshop to a different location," Evie wondered aloud.

"No way," Rick said. "He didn't have the time or resources to accomplish something like that."

"So are you saying what I think you're saying?" asked Evie.

"I'm saying that there's someone else on this continent."

Rick led the way across the spongy terrain. Sprout followed along at his side. "Aw, Rick, if y'all got rustlers trespassing on your continent, then they're gonna be in for a rude surprise when I acquaint them with my lasso."

The problem was that Rick didn't think a lasso would be enough to handle whoever had built these other buildings. On the kids' past adventures they had Dad or Mom, or at least 2-Tor, to protect them. Now they were on their own. Mom had been right all along. It was stupid and dangerous to go off without supervision.

"Everyone be quiet," Rick cautioned the others. "We don't know what we're dealing with yet."

Evie walked behind Sprout, shoulders back, hands at the ready. "I'm not afraid of any trespassers. Whoever's on our continent is going to regret bumping into me."

"This is serious, Evie," Rick snapped. He'd been trying to be a little less belligerent toward her ever since they'd headed off in the direction of the buildings, but then she had to go and be her usual bullheaded self. "Quit pretending to act tough. It's that kind of attitude that lost the super root and got us in this mess." There were enough risks in creating a new continent. They couldn't afford to have Evie take unnecessary ones.

As they reached the top of the next hill, they looked into the valley below and saw that the buildings were more than just random structures—they were a new settlement. Men in dark suits patrolled the area, armed with icetinguishers and stern faces. Each building was labeled with a sign written in a blocky font: "Paperwork Depository"; "Regulation Station;" "Hovership Permit Parking: *Park your permits here!*"

"It's—it's Winterpole," Evie stammered. "They're not supposed to be here! They don't have jurisdiction."

Rick shrugged. "They must have found a way around that."

Evie shifted on the rocky hilltop. "What do you think they did with Dad and 2-Tor?"

"Well I can answer at least part of that last one," Sprout said. "2-Tor. He's y'all's big bird thing, I reckon. Yeah?"

"That's right," Evie nodded. "How'd you know?"

Sprout pointed to an open plaza in the center of the settlement, where a big ice sculpture stood on a deactivated hoversled, guarded by two armed agents in suits. At first glance Rick had assumed it was a shrine to cold weather erected as a result of Winterpole's weird obsession with its namesake season, but on closer inspection, he could see something inside the ice. A beak. The tip of a black feather.

"2-Tor!" Rick gasped.

"What? Trapped in the ice?" Evie rushed toward the settlement. "We have to save him!"

"Evie, wait!" Rick tackled her before she could get too far ahead. They tumbled to the ground, sending Rick's glasses flying. Sprout laughed uproariously.

"Get off me!" Evie shoved Rick away. "2-Tor is in trouble!"

"That Winterpole camp is crawling with guards. Don't you get it? They'd freeze you in two seconds, and then Sprout and I would have to rescue you *and* 2-Tor."

"You don't know that," Evie said.

Sprout tipped back his hat. "I think Rick is right, Evie. We gotta be cool as cucumbers if we want to save y'all's friend."

"And how are we going to do that?" Evie asked.

With an encouraging smile, Sprout said, "Trust me. There's a plan growing in my head, and I'm ready to harvest it."

11

NIGHT FELL LIKE A HEAVY BLANKET OVER THE EIGHTH CONTINENT. OUT IN THE MIDDLE OF THE ocean, far from civilization and its innumerable coughing engines, the continent floated alone in the dark, the only light the gleaming stars above.

The three kids lay flat on their stomachs, squinting in the dark to watch the Winterpole guards make their rounds. At this distance, the kids could see only bits of movement under the gas lamps that dotted the area. Two patrolmen circled the clearing and greeted a third in front of the barracks. Then, just as Sprout had predicted, the three guards dispersed—two went into the barracks where the agents slept, leaving just one to patrol the clearing.

"Finally!" Evie breathed a sigh of relief.

"Okay." Rick turned to face Evie and Sprout. "That's as safe as it's gonna get. Sprout, you ready to create your diversion?"

"Hoo-wee! You bet your broccoli, Rick."

"Good. You'll loop to the north side of the compound and

do what we talked about. Evie and I will crawl down to the western edge and get into position. Assuming the diversion works, we'll make a break for 2-Tor and activate the hover-sled. Remember to get out of there as fast as you can once we're done. Rendezvous at the *Roost*. Okay, Sprout? Sprout?"

The little cowboy had taken off. He was hunched over and running at a gallop toward the paperwork depository they'd noticed earlier.

Rick shook his head in disbelief. "That kid is crazy."

"Crazy cool!" Evie pulled Rick to his feet. "Come on, Ricky. It's robot-rescue time."

"2-Tor is an organic mutated crow now," Rick whispered as his sister led him across the terrain.

They crept down to a line of sheds along the edge of the compound and pressed against the prefabricated walls. They sidled along to the edge of the wall and then peered around the corner. Rick squinted into the darkness. Evie pulled him back before he was seen.

"The guard is right there," Rick whispered.

For several tense, quiet moments, they waited.

Evie pulled on Rick's shirt. "Isn't he supposed to patrol the whole compound? Why is he staying in one spot?"

"I don't know," Rick hissed. "Maybe he's suspicious that some noisy, nosy girl is going to try to break in."

Evie scowled. "Well where is Sprout with his diversion?"

Before Rick could reply, the paperwork depository exploded. A column of flame burst into the air like an erupting volcano. Scraps of fiery legal documents fluttered like dizzy comets.

"Oh," Evie said. "There it is."

The guard on patrol shouted in dismay and sprinted away in the direction of the explosion.

"I expected something a little more subtle," Evie said. "But wow. It worked."

"Yeah but . . ." Rick pointed at the barracks. A flood of other agents poured out, struggling into their uniforms and fumbling with icetinguishers. "Sprout woke up the entire compound."

"Oh, I see," Evie said. Then, darting around the corner of the shed, she added, "Well, come on! Don't want to waste a good diversion."

As Evie was about to enter the central clearing, Rick grabbed her and pulled her back. Just in time, too. A trio of agents crossed in front of the sheds at a fast clip. When the coast was clear, Rick and Evie ran to where 2-Tor's ice prison was resting on the hoversled.

Rick circled to the back of the sled, which was a slightly curved bed of shiny metal, about the size of a picnic table. After popping open the control panel, Rick started fiddling with the buttons. He powered up the hoversled without much trouble, and soon the engine was humming. It lifted the sled into the air, buffeting it on an invisible cushion of energy three feet off the ground.

The floating block of ice drew the attention of a half-dozen Winterpole agents, who were on their way to the burning depository. Their faces turned angry.

"Quick, Rick, hop on!" Evie shoved him into the bed of the hoversled.

"Wait!" Rick shouted. "The controls are very delicate."

This revelation didn't stop Evie. She punched the controls as hard as she could.

Evie clung to the hoversled as it rocketed through the pack of agents, sending them all in different directions. The sled veered upward over the roof of one of the sheds and soared into the dark.

From her high vantage point, Evie could see the agents at the north end of the compound shouting orders to each other and spraying the burning rubble of the depository with their icetinguishers. It then occurred to Evie that the hover engine on the sled did not have the power to keep them this high for very long, or even for any time at all.

As if sensing Evie's realization, the hoversled dropped. The kids screamed as it fell through the air. Then, *WHUMP!* The sled slammed into the mottled ground with a loud thud. But still the engine kept fighting. They bounced across the surface of the eighth continent until the hoversled regained enough altitude to carry the two kids and their 2-Tor-shaped cargo at a steady pace. Judging by the shouts behind them, it was clear the Winterpole agents were organizing a search party to go after the stolen hoversled, but it would not be easy to track them down in the darkness.

Using Rick's pocket tablet as a guide, they navigated their way back to the *Roost*, where Sprout was waiting for them. The little pyromaniac was carrying a blazing torch of rolled up paperwork, which cast jagged shadows against his face, illuminating his mischievous grin. His eyes went wide when he saw the size of the frozen 2-Tor up close.

"That there ice cube is gonna need a mighty big drink."

It wasn't long before Sprout and the Lanes had built a fire around the base of 2-Tor's frozen cell, using treated wood stored in the hull of the *Roost* for emergencies. Evie watched the coals spit with each drop of water that dripped off the block of ice, kicking embers up among the stars.

They couldn't leave the continent until 2-Tor defrosted. Sprout produced a bag of red beets from his satchel. They skewered the beets on sticks and roasted them over the fire like marshmallows. The beets actually tasted pretty good.

Her stomach full of root vegetables, Evie leaned back and thought about all the wonderful evenings when her father had brought out his telescope and stargazed with her and Rick. But thinking about these happy memories only hurt Evie's heart. Her mother was under arrest, her father was missing, and Rick hated her for losing the super root. Hard to believe that only a day ago she'd been enjoying her happy ending.

While Evie reflected, Sprout and Rick huddled over Rick's Game Zinger, their faces aglow in the red light of the fire and the blue light of the screen.

"What are you two looking at?" Evie asked, trying to rub a beet juice stain off her finger. The boys were pointing at little blobs on the screen and whispering.

Sprout looked up. "Rick's showing me the plan for the eighth continent settlement."

"*The* plan?" Evie scowled. "I didn't realize we had agreed on a plan."

Rick smiled innocently. That look made Evie want to throw a roasted beet at him. "I showed him my rendering of the layout. I just added a hydroponic lab. That'll help us grow fresh produce until we can conduct tests to determine how arable the land is. You see, with hydroponics, you grow plants using mineral nutrient solutions, so you don't need to use soil."

"It's the best darn way to grow plants I've ever seen!" Sprout added.

"I know what hydroponics are," Evie said. "But Sprout, we're not building a science dictatorship like Rick wants."

Rick glared. "It's not a dictatorship. The governing body of Scitopia will be a small group of carefully vetted and selected Nobel Prize winners, geniuses, and entrepreneurs."

"So like your daddy, and maybe the Prof, too!" Sprout nodded his approval of this decision.

Evie was unimpressed. "And who's gonna select this small group of egos with zero oversight and total authority? You, Rick? That's a dictatorship! And furthermore, *Scitopia*? What kind of ridiculous name for a continent is that?"

"An awesome one," Rick said. "And I'm not a dictator. How can you say that? I'm a good person with good intentions. I'll make everyone who lives on the eighth continent happy. I'll only make decisions that will do what's best for them."

"You mean what you *think* is best for them, Your Highness."

Rick scowled. Sprout snorted.

"The eighth continent should be a democracy. It's fair. Everyone gets a vote in how the continent operates." As Evie spoke she glanced at her poor bird tutor, still encased in ice. "The public can decide where to live, how to eat, and what kind of scientific research they want to do."

"Well what if they want to pursue scientific research that doesn't interest us?"

"That's fine. It's their right to disagree."

"What if the first thing they vote for is forfeiting Dad to Winterpole? What if they want to research bombs like Mastercorp does?"

"What?" Evie could hear her voice growing more frustrated. "That goes totally against our philosophy for creating the eighth continent. They can't do that!"

"Sure they can." Rick had that stupid grin on his face again, the one he had when he was winning. "If it's a democracy, then they can do whatever they want."

"Well then I'll make sure no one with dumb ideas like that is allowed to live on the eighth continent."

"Oh ho ho! And who decides who can come and who can't, Evie? You?"

She realized he totally had her. Darn it. She hated when he did that.

Rick went on. "So now you have complete control of immigration to the eighth continent and you won't let anyone in unless they do what you say."

"That's not what I meant!"

"Why not?" Rick smiled. "I think it sounds like a great idea."

Sprout stood up to stretch his legs. "Y'all're carrying on like two cats in a sack. I say y'all should find some common ground. I sure wouldn't bicker so heatedly about philosophy and politics with any of my kin. At least, I wouldn't if I had any."

Evie frowned. "We're sorry, Sprout. We didn't mean to upset you."

"Yeah," Rick agreed.

"Aw, y'all're fine." Sprout approached the block of ice, which had shrunk considerably. The feathered tips of 2-Tor's wings were sticking out of the ice cube. Sprout picked up a burning log from the fire, careful not to touch the part of it that was hot. He held it in front of 2-Tor, close, so the orange flame licked the glassy surface.

Rick and Evie grabbed torches and joined Sprout, waving the torches over the ice and watching as it melted away. As they worked, they heard a hissing sound almost like a whistle. "What's that noise?" Rick asked, straining to hear the sound.

"I reckon it's this over here." Sprout pointed. The tip of 2-Tor's black beak had emerged from the quickly melting ice. The top and bottom of the beak were slightly parted, and he was whistling faintly, breathing, through the gap.

Rick heaved a sigh of relief. "He's alive!"

The remaining ice around 2-Tor's head continued to melt away. The kids leaned in close, listening to 2-Tor's hoarse whisper. "I . . . say . . . I . . . say . . ."

"2-Tor! 2-Tor!" Evie touched his beak. It was as cold as the ice that still encased the rest of his body. "Can you hear me?"

"I say! Do not shoot!"

"2-Tor, what are you talking about?" Evie said, her heart pounding. "We're not going to shoot you."

"I think he's having flashbacks of whatever happened to him before he was frozen," Rick explained. "Hurry, let's try to finish thawing him out as quickly as possible."

It took several more minutes to completely extract 2-Tor from the ice. They had to keep building up the fire to prevent the melting water from putting it out. Once 2-Tor was free, they dried him with towels from the *Roost* and wrapped him in warm blankets. He sat close to the fire, while the kids listened to his story.

"It was a most distressing turn of events. Your father and I were looking into purchasing a very large anchor to root the continent, but that most unpleasant gentleman Mister Snow arrived, with a contingent of his fellow agents."

"Winterpole," Rick muttered in disgust.

"They said they were going to take your father. But I do not know where. Back to Geneva? I am uncertain, and you know how irregular it is for me to be described that way."

"So it's settled," Evie said. "We have to break into Winterpole headquarters, again, and rescue Dad. What other choice do we have?"

"But what if he's not there?" Rick asked. "2-Tor doesn't know where they took him. Dad could be at the Prison at the

Pole for all we know, or any Winterpole facility. Wouldn't they assume their headquarters is the first place we would look for him? It might be a trap for us. And besides, even if we could magically discover where they were keeping him, what would we do once we got him out? The continent is still on a collision course with Australia. Winterpole would just arrest him again. They still have a presence here. Our only chance is to root the continent, so that we have a place to bring Dad once we free him."

Evie leaned against 2-Tor, feeling dejected. They'd *had* a way to root the eighth continent, but she had lost it.

Rick prattled on. "This time tomorrow, the collision will have already happened. Australia is in danger. Preventing its destruction has to be our number-one priority."

"I reckon I know a way to solve this here predicament," Sprout said. 2-Tor tilted his head curiously at the young boy. The big crow clearly appreciated the assistance Sprout had provided in the rescue operation. Sprout took a deep breath. "What if we look for a replacement root?"

"But I thought you said that Professor Doran didn't have any more roots?" Evie asked, her pulse rising. Sprout's last suggestion sounded too good to be true.

"I said that *Professor Doran* didn't have any more. But, remember, the old prof didn't invent the Amazonian Super Root; he just collected one. He told me that he found it in a rainforest in northern Brazil."

"Does that mean that we could really locate another?" Rick sounded as shocked as Evie felt.

Sprout smiled. "I'll need the *Roost*'s GPS to pinpoint the exact area, but it shouldn't be too much trouble."

Evie felt her hopes rise. Another scavenger hunt was about to begin—this time for a reclusive root.

THE NEXT MORNING, THE *ROOST* WAS ON ITS WAY TO THE AMAZON RAINFOREST BEFORE RICK HAD time to pick the sleep gunk out of his eyes. He hunched over the hovership's controls, struggling to stay awake. Normally, 2-Tor would have been piloting, but the bird's new organic wings lacked the mechanical dexterity of his old robot body, so he couldn't grip the flight wheel. Meanwhile Sprout, Evie, and 2-Tor analyzed data from the *Roost's* scanners and orbital satellites to find the exact location of the super root.

Suddenly, the big blue blur of rushing water below them became the big green blur of rushing treetops. They reduced speed so Sprout could check the satellite data they had collected and compare it to the rainforest underneath them.

"Hoo-wee!" the little cowboy shouted, startling the others. "I see the grove right down there!"

Rick felt a warm rush of excitement. He didn't know where they'd be without Sprout. He knew so much about the super root and other plants, not to mention he was pretty good in a rescue operation. Rick hoped Sprout liked him as much as he liked Sprout.

Ahead, there was a round hole in the tree cover about the size of a football stadium. They flew over the hole, soaring past thick tangled vines.

"The *Roost*'s scanners indicate we have arrived at the correct destination," 2-Tor observed.

Shaking Rick's shoulder to get his attention, Evie said, "So let's go! Bring the *Roost* in for a landing."

"Come on, Evie, I can't! If I try to land the *Roost* in the glade the hover engines might burn up every super root down there."

"Rick's right," Sprout agreed. "I reckon we should find another place to land and approach the grove on foot."

"Sheesh!" Evie threw up her hands in frustration. "Nobody ever sides with me."

They found a small gap in the tree canopy a couple miles south of the grove, taking advantage of natural camouflage provided by the local flora. The leaves and bark of the *Roost* were different colors from those of the surrounding trees, but a person would have to be highly observant to notice anything amiss.

"Stay focused," Rick urged them as they packed canteens, backpacks, and other standard adventuring provisions. "If we don't find the super root and anchor the eighth continent by sunset, it will be too late."

"Thanks for the words of comfort, Rick," Evie said sarcastically.

Rick ignored her jab, and the four travelers left the *Roost* behind. Sprout led the way, hacking through the dense undergrowth.

A stentorian roar filled Rick's ears—the sound of billions of insects singing their songs. The trees were titans, and their leaves applauded each gust of wind. The howls and screeches of countless animals came from all around him. "Are we safe walking around like this?" he asked.

Sprout slashed through a clump of knotted branches, opening a path. "Sure! Why, any animals out here are more scared of us than we are of them. You just gotta watch out for snakes."

Rick nodded. "Keep your eyes on the ground. Got it."

"Naw, they hang out in the trees up there. Once in a while they'll drop right on your head!"

Rick ducked reflexively. Evie giggled.

2-Tor raised a feathery finger in the air. "If I recall correctly, the most dangerous animal in the Amazon is the mosquito."

Rubbing his arms worriedly, Rick thought, *Don't eat me, Mister Mosquito. I taste terrible. I swear.*

Sprout hacked away at a dense thicket. Evie helped pull away the fallen vines. The boy said, "Here's an interesting riddle. What animal has destroyed more lives in the Amazon than any other?"

"Hmm . . ." Evie rubbed her chin. "Flesh-eating piranhas?"

Rick said, "I'm going to go with 2-Tor and say mosquitoes."

"Wrong!" Sprout sliced through the wall of roots, exposing a clearing. "The answer is—"

"Fore!"

A high-speed white projectile flew past them, nearly knocking Sprout's head off. The golf ball bounced across the ground and rolled into a sand trap.

Golf ball? Sand trap? Rick slapped his cheek a few times to make sure he wasn't dreaming.

Pristine buzz-cut grass stretched before them. To their left was a golf green, complete with a skinny flag sticking out of the hole. In the distance, beyond the golf course, there was an expanse of pastel buildings, pinks and turquoises and yellows, tall hotels and condominiums. At the center of it all was a gray spire, like the tower of a medieval castle. The whole area, castle included, was surrounded by the forested wall of the Amazon jungle.

Rick was about to ask, *What is this place?* when he heard: "Dagnabbit! Them kids got in the way of my shot! I'm taking a mulligan."

"You already took three mulligans, Scotty. You can't take another one."

"Hah? Herb, if those kids blocked your shot, you'd make us go back to the front nine and give me a five-stroke penalty."

Rick, Evie, and Sprout watched as two old men marched up the fairway to the green. The first was a short bald man in a flannel shirt and navy suspenders who fanned himself with a scottish flat cap, which seemed much too hot to wear in the sweltering jungle. The other was a big man with an enormous gut, a shock of white hair, and a nose like a stoplight. His trousers were so brightly colored that they hurt Rick's eyes. Following behind the two men were two bags of golf clubs on robotic plastic pink chicken legs. The robo-bags walked close behind their owners.

"Hey, Scotty, you know I think these kids might've come out of the jungle!"

"The jungle? That's crazy. Hey, you kids, did you come out of the jungle?"

The Lane siblings stared stupidly at the two old men. Sprout grinned, looking like he was getting a kick out of the whole thing.

Herb shook his golf club at them. "Hey, you kids! Do I have to bop you with my five-iron? Wake up!"

"Wha . . . what is this place?" Rick asked.

"This place? Are you kidding?" Herb snorted in offense. "Why, this is New Boca!"

Evie raised an eyebrow. "New . . . Boca?"

"Yeah. You know. Like *Boca Raton*. What are you, deaf?"

"Hah?" Scotty put a hand to the side of his head.

Herb shouted in Scotty's ear. "I said they're deaf, Scotty. The kids are deaf."

Scotty adjusted his hearing aid. "The kid's a chef? Good, the food here is terrible."

The white-haired man started to grimace but then his robo-bag nudged him. He pulled out a putter and stepped onto the green. He pointed with his club at the town beyond the golf course. "You gotta be over sixty-five to live in New Boca, but I'm sure you can find water and supplies down in the shopping district. Now shoo, rug rats. We gotta finish our game or I'll miss the early-bird special."

"Hah? The dirty nerd vessel?"

"Scotty, that doesn't even make any sense. Meanwhile your golf bag looks like it's about to lay an egg. Grab your sand wedge and take your shot."

"The chef kid's making a sandwich? Good, I'm hungry."

"Uh, I think we're going to get going," Rick said. But the two men just continued bickering and so the bird, the cowboy, and the brother and sister tiptoed away from the putting green and into New Boca.

The streets smelled of fresh asphalt and the buildings looked brand new, as if the whole thing had sprung up overnight. Highly chlorinated fountains stood smack in the middle of each intersection, shooting water into the air. Old ladies roamed in packs, power-walking in nylon tracksuits that matched the pastel buildings around them.

A group of serving-bots rolled past pushing food carts. Rick thought about snatching some food off the carts. He was starving. But one look at the food—tuna noodle casserole, Metamucil, and big glass candy dishes filled with a variety of prescription medications—changed his mind.

The storefronts they passed were similarly themed. Here was the yarn store. There was the pet store (all it sold was cat food and kitty litter). At the end of the road was a store where you could rent black-and-white movies on video cassette.

"This place is weird," Sprout observed.

"Yeah, I know," Rick replied. "It's almost like it fell from the sky."

"Look!" Evie yelled, pointing as she ran over to a big wooden sign. Letters had been carved and then painted pink and gold. It read: "Welcome to NEW BOCA . . . A development of the Condo Corporation."

"Condo Corp? Oh man!" Rick adjusted his glasses in irritation. "What is up with those people? And why are they so obsessed with Florida?"

"I can't even reckon how many trees they must have chopped down to build this place." Sprout kicked the sidewalk.

2-Tor squawked. "According to my calculations, more than sixty thousand flowering plants and trees were cut down to make room for this community."

Rick took out his pocket tablet and examined the digital map. "The data I've gathered here says the glade with the super root is on the other side of New Boca."

Evie stomped her foot. "If Condo Corp messed with the super root, I am gonna mess with them. *Wha-bam!*"

"Vesuvia is in prison," Rick said. "So who is running Condo Corp now?"

"I dunno," Evie replied, "but first things first: How do we get to the super root?"

"We could try to skirt around the perimeter of the town," Rick suggested. "Stick to less-densely populated areas."

A deep, harsh growl from behind them interrupted this line of thought. Rick turned to see a nine-foot-tall pink plastic gorilla looming. He wore a rather snazzy tuxedo, custom-fitted to his Buick-sized frame, and carried a dainty plate piled high with half-sour pickles.

"Oh!" Evie yelped, startled by his arrival. "Hello. Nice monkey."

The robot gorilla roared. He dropped the pickles and raised his hands, which morphed into whirling circular saws before their eyes. The blades screamed like anguished goats.

"Not nice monkey! Not nice monkey!" Evie took off down the street.

Rick thought this was the best idea she'd had in a while. He ran after her. A group of old ladies saw the stampeding robo-gorilla and power-walked for cover.

At the end of the road Rick, Evie, Sprout, and 2-Tor darted into a corner boutique. Jeweled necklaces were mounted on the walls. Crystal chandeliers hung from the ceiling. And little crystal animals stood proudly in display cases, their gem eyes sparkling.

The robo-gorilla sliced the door in half and forced his way inside, his broad shoulders knocking out big chunks of the doorframe and wall.

"You know, I know the head of Condo Corp, and she's not gonna be too happy to find out that you ruined one of her precious developments," Evie taunted, clearly hoping that the gorilla would be able to see reason.

He didn't.

Instead, he smashed the figurines into glitter, sent the

necklaces flying off the walls, and tore a chandelier free of its mounting.

"Guess he hasn't met Vesuvia, huh?" Evie mused.

Rick didn't have a chance to mention that he wondered if perhaps Vesuvia had been the one to send the gorilla in the first place—it was pink after all—because before he knew it, the three of them burst through the exit door at the back of the store and stopped short.

A woman stood before them. She was young but hard-featured. Over her Kevlar bulletproof vest and black commando pants she wore a wrinkly gray cloak, which on closer inspection Rick realized was made out of the hide of an elephant. She was holding a bowzooka, a dangerous weapon that was a mix between a crossbow and a shotgun.

Rick had seen people like this before. A poacher. A kind of hunter who shot and collected rare animals illegally. But behind them, the gorilla was sawing through the exit door. This poacher was their only hope.

"Please, Miss," Rick begged the silent woman. "You've gotta help us. This robot's after us. It's trying to chop us up."

She looked at the three children before her. The robot behind them was more than halfway through the door. Her gaze shifted to the tall black crow standing upright before them.

Without a word, she fired her bowzooka.

Dozens of tranquilizer darts flew from the bow in a spray, each needle taking the shape of a mosquito. Several caught 2-Tor in the breast and side as he instinctively shielded Evie with his wing. Sprout dropped to the ground. Evie cried, "Hey, don't shyaaarrrgh . . ." as another blast caught her with a couple darts. She and 2-Tor fell to the floor and were still.

Something pinched Rick's arm. He looked down and saw one of the darts embedded in his shoulder. He pulled it out and stared at it. A second later it became clear that while the dart was staying the same distance away, fresh black asphalt was getting closer. He landed hard on his face.

Rick rolled over to see Sprout leap from the ground like a tiger from the brush. He knocked the bowzooka up, sending a blast of darts into the air. The woman growled and Sprout ripped the bowzooka from her hands. He swung it, attempting to hit her in the face, but she was too quick. She leaned back, let the butt of the weapon swish by, and then lunged at Sprout, catching him with an elbow to the jaw.

Dazed, Sprout stumbled backward. She grabbed him by the shoulders and kneed him in the chest. His wind gone, Sprout dropped to his knees.

The woman stripped the bowzooka from his loose grip and struck him with it in the back of the head. Sprout collapsed in a heap, unconscious.

Rick wanted to get up. To help. To fight. But he couldn't. His whole body was numb. His vision was dark and fuzzy. Unconsciousness sounded like the next-best idea.

13

EVIE WOKE TO A HEADACHE LIKE SOMEONE HAD FORCE-FED HER TEN GALLONS OF ICE CREAM AND only now was the brain freeze catching up with her. She was lying on her back, staring up at a ceiling brightly painted to look like a summer sky, with puffy white clouds and a smiling yellow sun. The sky was moving—no, wait—*Evie* was moving.

She looked around as her vision cleared. She was sitting in a little inflatable boat shaped like a pink hippopotamus. The boat floated on an indoor lake that looked like it had been built inside a baby's playroom, complete with paintings of castles and fields. Two other hippo boats floated nearby. Evie paddled over to one with her hands. The water was as warm as a bath.

She nudged the boat's passenger. "Sprout. Sprout, hey. Wake up."

The boy stirred, rubbing his forehead. "Oof. I feel like some varmint kicked up a fire ant mound inside my brain."

"Ditto," Evie said. "Rick! You awake?"

"Barely," he muttered, his red hair appearing over the rump of the third hippo boat. "Where's 2-Tor?"

Sprout shrugged. "I reckon he's asking the same thing about us."

"I'm asking the same thing about us!" Evie said.

Sprout paddled toward the exit, where an arched hallway led off from the playroom. The water flowed down the passage in a stream. "I ain't sure what this place is, but I'd bet you dollars to durians if we go this way we'll find out."

Rick and Evie followed him in their inflatable boats, the water current pulling them in the very direction they wanted to travel.

Evie sighed at the memory of their bigger mission. "We're sort of like the eighth continent, you know? Getting pulled this way and that."

"Yeah, but at least we're not about to crash into Australia," Rick reminded her. "Speaking of which—" He pulled out his pocket tablet and inspected the waterproof device. "We have less than a day left to stop the two continents from colliding."

Evie gulped. She couldn't believe that the countdown was more than half over. If only she hadn't lost the first super root, they'd have anchored the continent by now and rescued their parents.

The sound of blaring music interrupted Evie's thoughts. "It's like the soundtrack to an old Hollywood musical," she muttered to herself, expecting to see dozens of long-legged dancers in diamond-encrusted swim caps forming kaleidoscopic designs in the water. But as they were propelled into yet another indoor lake all she saw was more inflatable animals—a crocodile here, a stingray there—all pink, and without occupants. Was there no one else in this puffy pastel heaven?

"I say, one more meager handful. It is all I ask."

"That sounds like 2-Tor!" Evie said.

The voice grew louder. "Evelyn? Is that you? Over here!"

Evie slipped out of her boat and waded to the edge of the lake. The ground, the walls, everything in this place had the give of an inflatable bouncy castle. Maybe it *was* an inflatable bouncy castle? Pretty cool. It must have been that tall castle spire she had seen from the golf course, in the middle of New Boca.

She slipped several times climbing out of the lake, but then managed to beach herself, her soggy shoes squeaking on the plastic. Rick and Sprout paddled over to her and climbed out of the water, dripping everywhere.

2-Tor stood a few dozen yards away. He wore a collar around his neck that chained him to an inflatable palm tree. On a pedestal in front of him was a silver tray piled high with wriggling earthworms, and at his side was the woman poacher from the jungle. She turned to look at the three children and tossed a fistful of worms at 2-Tor, who snatched them out of the air with his beak, gobbling them eagerly.

"Good evening, children!" 2-Tor said with a full mouth, a breach of manners he would have reprimanded Evie for, she was certain. "This is Elizabeth, otherwise known as the Big Game Huntress, one of the most violent and devious poachers on the planet. She's wanted by the authorities in over two dozen nations."

"A pleasure," the Big Game Huntress said, sounding like she was trying out to be a contestant in the *America's Most Apathetic* competition.

Evie's forehead wrinkled in confusion. "2-Tor, you're chained up. Why do you sound so happy?"

The bird swallowed loudly. "She is serving me all the worms I can eat. Have you ever had worms, Evelyn? They're delicious!"

"Let him go," Rick demanded, wearing his serious face.

The Big Game Huntress gave a nasty cackle. "What? Never. This is the first I've ever seen a specimen like this. He's exquisite. You hear that, bird? Exquisite. He's the prize of my collection. You can't have him."

Evie wasn't afraid. "We'll take him by force if we have to."

"Oh yeah? Force? How'd that work out for your friend last time?"

Sprout rubbed the big knot on the back of his head ruefully.

"Go ahead, kids. Try me. Next time I'll make you sleep longer. A *lot* longer. Ya dig?"

A sweet voice interrupted. "Oh, will you leave those little dears alone? Hello, my darlings. Please, have a cookie. Have two of every color."

A huge plastic flamingo in the lake turned to face them. The back of the flamingo was curved, forming an inflatable throne upon which the littlest old lady Evie had ever seen reclined. She was skinny as a stick. Her bright white hair fluffed above her wrinkly head like the mane of a Pomeranian. She wore bulbous sunglasses and a mottled nylon pink tracksuit that whistled when she moved. In her hand was a mug made from a hollowed-out coconut from which a straw, three wedges of pineapple, and seven paper umbrellas stuck out.

The old lady pushed an inflatable turtle with a plate of cookies on its back across the water. It ran aground near Sprout, who passed the plate to Evie. "Y'all know I ain't much for sweets."

"Of course, dear. I understand." The old lady shooed the Big Game Huntress away. "Elizabeth, be a dear and fetch Mister Sanchez a wheatgrass smoothie. We take our smoothies very seriously around here."

The Big Game Huntress stalked away with a gray cloud over her, muttering, "I never should have hunted penguins at that Condo Corp ski resort and fallen in with these people. Sure, the money's good, but give me a break. I've punched a tiger—I didn't take this job to wait on cubs."

Sprout bowed his head to the old woman. "That's mighty nice of you, ma'am. I thank you kindly."

"Oooh! Such nice manners. You were raised right, young man."

"How do you know our names?" Rick asked suspiciously.

The old woman raised her sunglasses to inspect Rick

with her sharp blue eyes. "I'm a very resourceful lady. One must be, to remain the super secret Chairwoman of the Board of the Condo Corporation."

Evie gawked in disbelief. "Then you're . . ."

"Venoma Condolini, at your service. But you can call me Grandma. Or Gran. Most of my grandchildren call me Granny."

Still trying to puzzle it out, Evie said, "Grandma . . . Condolini? Then Vesuvia is your . . ."

Grandma Condolini's face brightened at the mention of Vesuvia's name. It was the first time Evie had ever seen anyone do so. "Oh! You know my granddaughter?"

She insisted the children have a seat and eat a cookie, and then another, and then have a nice chat. They pulled off their shoes and socks, rolled up their pant legs, and dangled their feet in the warm water. The Big Game Huntress came back scowling with a tall glass of green sludge, which Sprout slurped joyously.

"You must forgive my chief of security," Grandma Condolini explained. "She is quite humorless, but very good at her many jobs—catching trespassers, for instance. Yes, don't bother explaining. We've been monitoring you ever since you landed your flying tree in my jungle."

"*Your* jungle?" Rick asked confrontationally.

"Why yes," Grandma Condolini said. "I own all this land. That's why I chose it as the place to build New Boca." She held out her arms, as if taking in the enormous bouncy chamber around them. "Isn't it just grand?"

"This place is weird," Evie said.

Grandma Condolini pointed a finger at her. "You could do with a lesson in manners from your friend here, little missy. Do not disrespect your elders. Now, what exactly are you doing here?"

"Why should we tell you?" Evie folded her arms over her chest. She wasn't about to be polite to Vesuvia's grandmother, of all people.

"Why? Why, because if I don't know, then how can I help you?"

"Help us?" Rick sounded as confused as Evie for once. "You expect us to believe *you* would help *us*? You chopped up the rainforest to build this place. A robot gorilla attacked us in *your town*. And your granddaughter is a complete psychopath."

Grandma Condolini nodded. "Ah. Now I see why we have gotten off on the wrong orthopedically corrected foot. How did Vesuvia wrong you?"

"You mean besides tormenting me at school?" Evie asked.

"And kidnapping us?" Rick added.

"And sinking our submarine and killing our friend?" Evie felt a deep pain in her heart remembering the untimely death of her father's former research partner, Doctor Grant.

With a heavy sigh, Grandma Condolini said, "Oh dear me. That girl. She really is a nightmare."

Evie stopped short. "She . . . what?"

"It pains me to admit it, but Vesuvia has always been a rotten strawberry, ever since she was little. Maybe it's the Piffle in her. Condolini women have always possessed impeccable manners. For a long time Vesuvia's behavior wasn't so bad, until last year when her mother disappeared. You see, I was retiring, to rest after so many years in the big chair, even bigger than my flamingo lounger, and to focus on my pet project, *New Boca Raton.*

"My daughter, Viola, had been groomed since birth to take over for me when the time came. You see, a Condolini woman *must* run Condo Corp. That is the way it has always been. That is the way it must be. And then one day, my daughter vanished. I had hoped that once she was in control of the company, my daughter would raise Vesuvia to be better behaved, to be like one of us, so that one day she too could claim the crown of Condo Corp. But when Viola disappeared, I had no other choice. A Condolini woman *must* run Condo Corp. And so I made my granddaughter the super-secret CEO. Now, I know Vesuvia is . . ."

"Cruel?" Evie offered.

"Evil?" Rick suggested.

"Pure evil?" Evie amended.

Grandma Condolini sighed. "But Condolini women have served the ideals of our family for generations. When the big earthquake flattened San Francisco in 1906, who made houses on the cheap? Us. After the *blitzkrieg*, who rebuilt London? We did. When the sea level rose and drowned Venice, who built New Lido *pro bono* so that every refugee had a place to stay for free? That wasn't Lane Industries, children. That was me."

"Some would call that profiteering," Evie said.

The old woman glared. "Some would not be the millions of people who wouldn't have roofs over their heads if not for Condo Corp. We intend to house the whole human race one day. No one is pure evil, children. I suggest you do not harbor that assumption."

Evie looked into her brother's eyes. Everything he wanted to say was written all over his face, as clearly as the time he fell asleep watching TV and she took a black permanent marker and actually wrote all over his face. He wanted to believe her story, even if he didn't. He wanted to trust Grandma Condolini, even if he couldn't. They needed her help if they were going to get the super root.

Evie, for one, wasn't buying what Grandma was selling. Sure, she seemed like a sweet old lady, but she was the mother brain of Condo Corp. How sweet could she be?

Rick told Grandma Condolini the story of how Vesuvia's Piffle Pink Patrol attacked the eighth continent and knocked it onto a collision course with Australia. He described the super root they needed to anchor the continent, and the location of the glade where it grew on Condo Corp's property.

Grandma Condolini listened carefully to everything he said and at last nodded. "Children, it is my sincerest pleasure to help you. Vesuvia must have programmed her robots to attack you if she was out of contact for a given amount of time. Just dreadful. Well, I hope by giving you access to this super root, it can go a little way toward making up for all the trouble my granddaughter has caused you."

Sprout grinned. "I reckon that's the best news we've heard all day!"

"But . . ." Grandma Condolini said.

There was always a *but*.

"But if I am going to give you a plant from my private property, I am going to need you to give me something in return. Something very precious."

Evie looked over at 2-Tor, who was still chained to the fake palm tree, chowing down on earthworms. "You can't keep 2-Tor."

"No, not him!" Grandma Condolini said. "You see, my granddaughter may be evil, but she is still my granddaughter."

A look of clarity, followed by a look of terror, passed over Rick's face. "Oh no. Not that. Anything but that."

Grandma Condolini smiled her sweetest grandmother smile. "That's right. Before you can get the root, I'm going to need you to rescue Vesuvia from the Prison at the Pole."

TWO LONG LINES OF EMPLOYEES TRAILED THROUGH THE CORRIDORS OF WINTERPOLE Headquarters. In the line on the left, people were waiting to enter the Winterpole auditorium, where the evening's entertainment was about to begin. In the line on the right, employees waited to receive their permission slips to stand in the line on the left. At her mother's insistence, Diana had gotten in the first line early. Now, permission slip in hand, she was ushered into the auditorium.

Inside, she walked down the center aisle, past rows of red velvet seats. A curtain hung over the screen at the front of the large room. The auditorium was an old movie theater that evidently had not been renovated since the silent era. Murals of angels sounding trumpets, while standing in line for craft services, adorned the walls. Diana slumped into a chair and tried to relax. Her feelings on every eighth continent–related thing were so muddled, they were weighing her down. Winterpole had been acting like a bully, as bad as Vesuvia, and Diana's mom was a part of it. The Lanes were the victims, as weird as that sounded.

Benjamin Nagg sat down three seats over from Diana, looking meticulously put together in his trainee uniform. He immediately pulled out his pocket tablet and started playing *Animon Hunters*. Diana looked away to hide her smirk. She could not wait to see Benjamin get in trouble. Only Winterpole agents level three and higher could receive permission slips to use pocket tablets in the auditorium.

Sure enough, a few minutes later one of the agent ushers approached Benjamin. "Ahem, ahem. I don't suppose you have a permission slip to be using that tablet, do you, trainee?"

"Why of course I do," Benjamin said, smugly presenting a sheet of cyber paper. "Mister Skole awarded me with this for my exceptional performance in class." He glanced at Diana as the usher took the paper. "Here you go. I believe it's all in order."

The usher examined the glimmering parchment. "Very good, trainee. Keep up the hard work. You'll be as high a level as me in no time."

As the usher walked away, Benjamin muttered under his breath, "One can only dream. Good grief."

At last, with every seat full, the lights dimmed and the curtain parted. The screen turned on, revealing security camera footage from a small cell at the Prison at the Pole. In the center of the room was George Lane, frozen up to his neck in a block of ice. Unshaven and miserable, George ignored the camera crew and his surroundings. The rumor was that he hadn't said a word since his arrest.

Mister Snow stepped onto the stage at the front of the

auditorium, casting his shadow across the movie screen. He held a microphone attached to a portable speaker. "Agents of Winterpole, welcome to a most momentous event. Director, can you hear me?"

"Good evening, agents!" The Director's voice boomed throughout the auditorium over the sound system. "I wish I could be there to witness this amusement in your presence, but alas, I must enjoy it on my private observation monitors."

Nodding with relief, Mister Snow continued. "The moving image you see behind me is coming to you live from cell Z-99 at the Prison at the Pole, where Winterpole's great enemy, the evil George Lane, is about to undergo the first stage of his punishment."

A metal contraption had been rigged over George's helpless form. A conveyor belt of metal buckets circled him.

"What we have devised we hope is to your satisfaction, Director. It is meant to be a testimony to our triumph, to be immortalized on magnetic tape and kept in a well-labeled filing cabinet in the basement of this very building."

The voice of the Director of Winterpole boomed again. "Proceed at a metered pace appropriate to the task."

Mister Snow shivered, as if this was the most delightful thing he had ever done. "Begin punishment!" he bellowed over the cheers of the agents in the auditorium.

They waited. The buckets circled. Everyone grew quiet. And then one of the buckets tipped over.

A flopping gray fish slipped out. It landed on George Lane's head with a wet smack, like a big sloppy kiss from an aunt who smells like tuna salad.

The laughter in the auditorium was deafening. Before it could die down another bucket tipped over and out came another fish. It pelted George on the head, leaving a fat bruise in its wake and fish juice all over his forehead. The auditorium shook with howls of amusement. Mister Snow beamed, his smile as wide as if he had just told some hilarious joke at a dinner party. Benjamin sounded like he was going to bust a gut. Diana really wished he would.

As the fishy avalanche continued, George remained silent. The camera zoomed in for a close up. Diana could see the pained look on his face. His expression made her feel sick.

Diana got up from her seat and hurried up the aisle to the exit. The laughter was all around her. That dark laughter. She didn't think it was funny at all.

Two ushers stopped her as she reached the doors. "Hey you, trainee. Where is your permission slip to leave the auditorium before the show is over?"

"I don't have a permission slip for that."

"You're not allowed to leave the auditorium without a permission slip."

Diana glared. "What if there is a fire?"

The usher dismissed her with a hand. "Our fire prevention methods are adequate."

She looked back at the screen. Now they were raining fish on George's head two at a time. Diana couldn't believe she was a part of this nasty circus.

"Please let me out. It's an emergency."

"Impossible," the usher replied.

Diana put her hands in her pockets, feeling her folded up permission slip to enter the auditorium. This gave her an idea.

She shrugged. "Why is it impossible? I got in here just fine without a permission slip."

The usher was aghast. "What?!"

"I don't have a permission slip to be in the auditorium," Diana lied.

"Outrageous! Horrendous!" The usher shook with anger. "Get out of here right this instant, you sneaky rule-breaking wretch. I will report you at once. How did you get past our sterling security team?"

As the ushers pushed her out of the auditorium, she pointed back at her seat. "Oh, my friend Benjamin snuck me in. He's right down there."

"Well we will deal with him!" the usher said confidently before slamming the door behind Diana.

In the hallway it was quiet and Diana was alone. She walked briskly through the deserted headquarters. Winterpole was supposed to be the good guys, protecting the environment and saving the world. None of this sat right with her. She had to talk to someone about it.

Minutes later, Diana found herself in front of her mother's office, knocking on the door. Her mother waved her in and told her to have a seat. She was on a call with the head of the legal department of some multinational corporation.

"Yes, yes, I read the report. . . . Well did you know the weaponized chemical bombs would leak when you built the transport boat? How much sea life are we talking about? . . . Global species collapse? That sounds like a lot. . . . Well, I'm glad you're concerned. It's always good to hear the groups we monitor expressing their concern for the environment. . . . It seems to me that you're in the clear on this one. You had permission slips to move weapons in that area. And oil spills happen in that region all the time. This is basically the same thing. Don't you worry. Local governments will raise taxes to pay for the cleanup and protect your subsidies. . . . I know! Your whole business model would break down if the average citizen didn't bail you out when you made a mistake . . . an innocent mistake. Yes, of course. Enjoy your vacation. . . . I *will* enjoy the opera tickets you sent. I'm so glad you remembered I love Wagner. Goodbye." Diana's mother pulled the headphone off her ear and set it on her desk. "Yes, and what do you want, Diana?"

"I just came from the auditorium."

"Oh that's good. How was the show?"

Diana shook her head, struggling to answer. She wanted to tell her mother what she expected to hear, but Mister Lane's punishment troubled her too much. "It doesn't feel right to be treating Mister Lane so cruelly. I know he needs to be punished for breaking the rules, but couldn't we come up with something a little more humane?"

Her mother rose from her chair and leaned across her desk. "George Lane did not simply 'break the rules'; he has violated countless Winterpole statutes. He has refused to acquire permission slips for anything. If it were up to me, his punishment would be much more severe. Your leniency disappoints me, Diana."

That was the worst thing Diana's mother could have said. She didn't want to be a disappointment. The whole reason she joined Winterpole in the first place was to make her mother happy. Diana's stomach scrunched up like a balled fist. It was scary to tell her mother the truth, but she had to do it. "I don't like it here, Mom. Everyone is so serious all the time. And mean. And the Director. What's up with that guy? Why does he talk so funny?"

"You fool!" Diana's mother cried out, a look of demented terror in her eyes. "Don't you *ever* question the Director. He is the Director. He—" She trailed off, smoothed down her uniform, and stepped around her desk, making her way to the door. She looked back at Diana. "Honestly, sometimes I don't know what you're thinking." She shut the door behind her, leaving Diana alone in the office.

Diana rubbed her cheek. She should have known better than to go to her mother for advice. No one understood how she felt. The people here were completely devoid of compassion.

Who would have thought Winterpole could be so cold?

RICK PULLED THE OARS WITH ALL HIS MIGHT, PROPELLING THEIR INFLATABLE RAFT THROUGH the choppy ocean. The mist was blizzard-thick. He squinted into the bleak gray vastness, fearful of every shadow.

"We should have taken the *Roost*," Evie said for the seventh time. But that was impossible. Grandma Condolini had told them the prison's sensors could detect any electronic signature in a five-mile radius. Rick's skinny arms were the only engine that could get close, and they would use the radio inside the lead-lined backpack they brought along to call Sprout for a pickup when it was time to flee the scene.

What they were about to do didn't sit right with Rick. He was no stranger to breaking Winterpole's nearly infinite list of rules and regulations, but this was different. He had always violated Winterpole's statutes for the greater good. This time it was to free a dangerous criminal.

"Vesuvia is just misguided," Grandma Condolini had said as they departed New Boca, leaving 2-Tor in the care of the Big Game Huntress as collateral. "I hope prison has cooled her temper. She may come out of the experience a different person."

Rick remained skeptical. He pulled up the zipper on his parka until it covered his chin. The next time he staged a prison break he swore he would pick one closer to the equator.

"Look, there it is!" Evie pointed ahead.

Rick squinted into the mist. The Prison at the Pole emerged, a white mountain on the black sea, a monument to frigid misery. Rick had always been taught that the location of this terrifying place was one of Winterpole's most carefully guarded secrets. But somehow Grandma Condolini had known where it was. A little bird had told her, she'd said.

As the enormous iceberg loomed ahead, Rick made out a number of mounted hoses on the rampart. Freeze rays. If they were detected now, he and his sister would be turned into a couple of ice cubes.

Evie squinted into the mist. "I have a visual on our point of entry. This is going to be fun."

"No, Evie. This is definitely not going to be fun," Rick said as he rowed.

"Sure it will!" Evie looked back at him. "Climbing. Sneaking. It's gonna be awesome! Sprout would find it fun."

Rick snorted. "It's obvious you don't know Sprout the way I do, or you would never say that."

"Psssshh. Yeah, right. I know Sprout so much better than you do. That's why we're friends."

"Just don't go bungling our mission again," Rick said, ignoring her. "In and out. No getting creative. No trouble."

The raft bumped against the icy exterior wall of the prison. Evie seized the raft's anchor and jammed it into the ice as Rick tucked the oars onto the raft. They each grabbed a pair of metal climbing picks and hoisted themselves out to begin their ascent.

Fifty feet up from the water, they stopped on a narrow ledge. A small hole no bigger than a loaf of bread had been cut out of the ice and covered with a grate of icicles.

Evie put her face close to the grate. "Hoo! What is that stench?"

"I don't know." Rick shivered. "I'm too cold to smell anything."

They attacked the grate with their climbing picks. The icicles shattered. Shards around the hole cracked and flaked away. As the hole widened, the stench inside became so pungent, even Rick's red runny nose got a whiff.

Hundreds of fish spilled out, flopping from ledge to ledge down into the ocean. Pressed against the wall to avoid the fishy deluge, Rick exchanged a perplexed look with his sister. "Let's go . . . I guess," he said.

They had expanded the hole enough to crawl through. Three feet in, the hole morphed into a circular tunnel like a sewer pipe, large enough for Rick and Evie to walk upright.

"Security seems light," Rick said, struggling to keep his balance. The floor was wet and slippery and stank of fish and waste.

Evie pinched her nose with two fingers. "I dunno. They're warding me off pretty well."

At the end of the tunnel was a ladder of curved metal bars embedded in the ice. A red hazard light provided the only illumination.

"All right, here we go." He climbed the ladder, hand over hand. The metal was so cold, he could feel it through his gloves.

The hatch at the top had a long handle. He pulled it slowly and quietly. The mechanism squeaked in protest. Taking a deep breath, Rick pushed the hatch open.

A dark hallway, which, like the others, was carved from ice, stretched out before him. Small alcoves with metal doors lined the hall. These must have been cells. No guards or security cameras were in sight.

Rick called down to his sister. "Evie, come on. The coast is clear."

They closed the hatch and crept down the hall. As they passed the rows of cell doors, Evie said, "Hey Rick, wait a second. I just thought of something. Dad's been missing all this time. And Winterpole was on *Evie's Paradise*."

"We're not calling the eighth continent that. But anyway, so what?"

"Well what if Winterpole captured Dad. Wouldn't they bring him here? Isn't that what they wanted all along?"

Rick glared at her. "Evie, what are you saying?"

"I'm saying he could be here in this very building. At the very least maybe if we hack into their systems we could find out where he is."

"I seem to remember the last time we were creeping around a Winterpole facility you got a similar idea and it nearly got us both killed!"

Evie rolled her eyes. "You're always bringing that up. Come on, Rick. There's a chance, right?"

Rick wanted to find his father more than anything. The responsibility of being the person in charge was stressing Rick out. The irony of this, considering how hard Rick always worked to *be* the one in charge, was not lost on him. But Dad would know how to fix all their problems, and he would put Rick at ease, as he so often did. Unfortunately, there was no proof he was here. And the Prison at the Pole wasn't like Winterpole Headquarters. Every moment they wasted, their lives were in danger.

Letting out a resigned sigh, Rick said, "Okay. We'll try it." This was not something he was excited to do, considering how much work they had already put into not being discovered, but if they wanted to be sure if Dad was in the Prison at the Pole or not, then there was only one way to find out. Arching his back, Rick let out his loudest bird call. "Koo ka-koo ka-KOO!!!" It was their family call, the one that, no matter what, would bring other Lanes running. "Koo ka-koo ka-KOO!!!"

Silence was the only reply.

After a long wait, Rick put a comforting hand on his sister's shoulder. "Forget it. Okay, Evie? Now let's go, in case some Winterpole guards heard us. We have a mission. Do you want to save the eighth continent or not?"

Evie gave in too. "Of course I do."

"Good. So where are we going next?"

Evie whispered, "Remember what Grandma Condolini said—they're keeping Vesuvia on the top floor with the other maximum security prisoners. We're going to have to find some stairs or an elevator."

"There's a sign for the stairs just down this hall," Rick said, pointing. "Let's check it ou—wah . . . ACHOO!" Rick panicked. "Uh, do you think anyone heard that?"

"Let's not wait to find out," Evie replied, pulling him into an alcove.

"Sorry, it was an accident," Rick said as soon as they were out of view.

"You *never* accept that excuse from me. You know, you wouldn't get colds like this if you ate more veggies."

Rick glared. Evie had chosen a heck of a time to pick a fight. "I eat plenty of vegetables. All I did was sneeze. You're the one who lost the super root and got us in this mess. And anyway, you never cared about eating greens until Sprout came along talking about how cool they are."

"That's not true. There isn't anything in the world more delicious than a green bean."

"You're a green bean."

"Then I guess I'm delicious!"

Rick sighed, once again at a loss due to his sister's immunity to logic and reason.

Fortunately, no one had come to investigate Rick's sneeze. Convinced the coast was clear, he and Evie moved quickly and quietly to the stairwell. They pushed through the door and ran up several flights of stairs.

When they reached the top floor, Evie knelt down and placed her ear against the doors.

"Hear anything?" Rick asked.

"Shh . . . something muffled. Give it a second."

They waited.

Finally, Rick couldn't contain himself. "You know, Sprout told me he likes my ideas for how to rule the eighth continent."

Evie glared. "Oh yeah? Well he told me he likes my ideas."

"He's *my* friend, Evie. He wouldn't say that to you."

"Well he did."

"Well you're lying!"

Evie snorted. "Whatever, Rick. If you think that's true, then you're not as much of a genius as you think you are."

Rick's face felt hot enough to melt the whole prison. He was about to tell his sister to stuff her face with green beans when she pushed open the doors a crack and said, "Okay, I think we're clear. Take a look."

Rick pressed his eye against the crack between the doors. Two big snowmen stood at the end of the hall. But there was something off about them. Something mechanical. And then the snowmen moved! As they turned and disappeared down another hall, Rick caught a glimpse of their faces. Where there should have been black coal for their eyes, there were blood-colored infrared lights.

Once they were sure no one was watching, Rick and

Evie moved into the hall. They started checking the cell numbers for Vesuvia: Z-100, Z-99, Z-98, Z-97.

As they neared the end of this latest hallway, the door to cell Z-99 hissed and slid open. Several Winterpole agents emerged, and Rick and Evie ducked into another alcove just in time.

"Nice work, crew," said the biggest man Rick had ever seen. Like the other prison guards, he was dressed in white instead of standard-issue black. "Good shoot," he told the other agents, who Rick now realized were carrying film equipment. "Take ten, then back to your posts."

The big man and the film crew walked away in the opposite direction from Rick and Evie. "That big guy must be the Polar Bear," Rick said, releasing a breath he hadn't realized he'd been holding. The Polar Bear was something else Grandma Condolini had warned them about. He was the warden of the Prison at the Pole and one of Winterpole's most fearsome agents. Rick did *not* want to cross paths with him.

"Why do you think they call him the Polar Bear?" Evie asked.

"I'm not sure. Maybe because he's almost as big as a bear."

"I hope that's the only reason," Evie said.

"Come on." Rick urged her to follow him to the next hallway. "Let's go rescue the pink princess."

A few minutes of cautious sneaking later, they found what they were looking for. A little corridor led off from the main hallway. At the far end was a single door. Carved into the ice beside it was the label Z-01. Vesuvia's room.

Evie's hand hovered over the open button next to the door. "Are we really going to do this?"

Rick frowned. "Do we have a choice?"

"Fair point," Evie replied, pushing the button.

The door slid open, but then the whole hallway went dark. Red warning lights flashed. Sirens blared. A voice came over the loudspeakers. "Attention. Attention. Escape attempt in progress in Sector Z."

"That wasn't my fault!" Evie said. "You totally can't blame me for that."

The loudspeaker voice again. "Repeat. Escape attempt in progress in Sector Z. Dispatch a Kill Team to investigate."

A Kill Team? That sounded worse than polar bears or snowman guards. Rick grabbed Evie and pulled her into the nearest cell, shutting the door behind them.

He jammed their climbing picks into the door, locking it. "That should hold them." As soon as he said this something heavy slammed into the door and growled. Then they heard someone or something pushing the open button. It clicked and hummed in struggle, but the door didn't budge. "Uh . . . for now."

Rick reached into their backpack and pulled out a flashlight. He switched it on and used the circle of light to explore the dark cell. Shadow icicles grew and twisted on the walls.

"Hello?!" he called out.

From back in the darkness, something groaned.

Rick and Evie followed the noise, searching the walls for the source of the sound.

Then, at the back of the cell, they found the cause. A girl had been frozen into the icy wall, so that only her head and hands stuck out. Her wiry blond hair draped like rags around her face. Her fingernails were dirty brown cat claws. She was too weak to shiver.

Evie approached the prisoner. "Vesuvia . . . Vesuvia . . . is that you?"

The girl raised her head. It *was* her. But she looked like a wind-up toy who'd had her spring ripped out. Her eyes struggled to focus on the two people before her. "E- . . . Eee . . ."

Evie stepped closer. "Vesuvia, it's me."

"Yuh . . . you . . ." Vesuvia muttered something inaudible.

"We're here," Evie said. "We're here to . . ." She struggled with the word. "We're here to rescue you."

Vesuvia swallowed and a look of pain crossed her face as she attempted to speak.

Timidly, Evie reached out and touched Vesuvia's hand. She put her ear close to her lips. "What is it, Vesuvia? What did you say?"

Vesuvia whispered. "I said . . . your shoes . . . are hideous."

"AAAAND I'M DONE. RICK, THIS WAS A FUN RESCUE MISSION AND ALL, BUT I'M OUT OF HERE. Let the snow cone enjoy her deluxe accommodations." Evie made for the exit. She'd have rather run from a million Winterpole agents than spend another infuriating minute with the Princess of Plight, Vesuvia Piffle.

Rick grabbed Evie by the hand. "Evie, wait! Remember why we're doing this."

The super root. Right. She watched as Rick opened their lead-lined backpack and withdrew a pair of flame-colored metal devices that Grandma Condolini had given them.

Rick flicked on the thermal torch. It glowed red as he held it in front of Vesuvia.

"Hey, what are you nerds doing? Get that away from me!"

Rick ignored her. The ice melted wherever he touched it with the torch. It worked much more quickly than the ordinary torches they'd used to free 2-Tor earlier, and pretty soon Vesuvia toppled to the floor like a wet rag. Her thin gray prison uniform clung to her in spots, leaving much of her purple and goose-bump-covered skin exposed. Vesuvia was always perfectly put together. It was weird to see her so wrung out.

Grunting with exertion, Rick lifted Vesuvia to a sitting position. "Your grandmother sent us here to rescue you. We're getting you out of here."

Vesuvia's eyes darted between the Lanes. "G- . . . Granny? Wha-wha-what is this, some kind of prank?"

Rick let go of her and put his hands under his arms to warm them up. "Evie, give her your hoodie. She's freezing."

"I'm not giving her my hoodie!"

"Evie, come on!"

"Ugh, it's fine," Vesuvia said through her chattering teeth. "I wouldn't be caught dead wearing that ratty old thing, anyway."

Something heavy slammed into the door to the cell. The door thrummed. From the other side, they heard a loud animal roar.

"The Polar Bear!" Vesuvia backed away as cracks appeared in the ice around the door. "Are you idiots crazy? The Polar Bear is right outside. He'll crush us faster than you can say 'super-secret CEO.' And that's the only way out of here. You *morons*!"

Evie turned on her thermal torch and held it against the floor of the ice cell, attempting to bore a hole into the floor. "Is speaking a requirement for a prison break? Can she not talk? Is that a rule we can make?"

Rick joined Evie with her melting efforts, but from the

way he kept glancing up at the door, she could tell that he thought Vesuvia—*Vesuvia!*—did have a point.

For every inch of ground she and Rick managed to melt, the Polar Bear slammed into the door at least four times. By this point, the cracks around the doorframe were too numerous to count.

"Faster, you fools! Hurry!" Vesuvia was standing now, shouting and looking down at them.

Soon they had a hole in the ice that was three feet across and ten feet down. Rick and Evie stared down into the hole, assessing the situation.

"We should be just another foot or two from breaking through into storage on the Y level," Rick said. "Evie, stay here with Vesuvia and then follow me down once I'm through."

"Be careful," Evie said, suddenly regretting some of the not-nice things she told him earlier.

Rick dove into the hole, his thermal torch held out in front of him. Once at the bottom, he used the tool to melt through the last bit of ice.

Wham! Wham! Wham! A big chunk of ice broke off the doorframe and shattered in the floor.

"Oh no!" Vesuvia shrieked. "The Polar Bear! It's the Polar Bear! He's coming through!"

Evie backed away from the door. "Vesuvia, chill out. He's a big dude, but he's just a guy."

"Just a—are you nuts?"

Down below, there was a tremendous crash and Rick

called out, "Evie, come on! I'm through!"

The cell door flew across the room and embedded in the wall. The white-haired warden stood before them. Now he wore massive cybernetic enhancements, including a shell of white reflective body armor, robotic gloves with steak-knife claws, and a helmet lined with steel teeth. Decked out in his gear, he looked like one thing and one thing only: a polar bear. Evie stared up at him in shock. She finally understood the reason for the man's reputation.

The guard knocked huge chunks of ice out of the wall as he pushed himself into the room. He growled, "Winterpole statutes prohibit prison breaks. I must apprehend you. Do not resist. I have a permission slip to maul you viciously."

Vesuvia screamed. Evie grabbed her by the hand. "Come on! Jump!"

The Polar Bear charged as the girls leaped into the hole. Evie braced her feet against the slick, icy surface to slow their descent. They landed just in time to see the Polar Bear jam his head into the hole. "Halt! Compliance is mandatory."

"We're not planning on stopping, right?" Vesuvia asked, holding out her hands, clearly expecting to be helped up.

"No, obviously not. We're not quitters." Evie climbed to her feet and looked around, ignoring Vesuvia's entreaties. The floor was covered with blocks of ice. Each block of ice contained a person, and each person was trapped: their bodies frozen like Vesuvia's had been, their frost-bitten faces contorted in agony.

"Please . . ." One of the men groaned. "I didn't mean to

use the forty-eight-cent stamps. I didn't know the price had gone up to forty-nine. Ohhhh . . ." The wails of the prisoners made Evie feel like spiders made of ice were crawling up her back.

"We have to help them!" she said. She ran to the old prisoner and started heating his shackles with the torch. "Rick, come on!" she yelled to her brother. "I can't free everyone by myself."

"Do not even think about listening to your idiot of a sister," Vesuvia shrieked. "If you don't keep digging, we're all gonna die!"

"Shut up, Vesuvia." Evie melted the ice away, but the prisoner was too disoriented to notice.

Rick shook his head. "Evie, she's right. There's no time."

"What?!"

The doors at the end of the cell block opened and two snowmen hopped into the room, their crimson eyes settling on Evie.

"Got it!" Rick screamed. "Evie, I broke through the floor. Let's go!"

Evie could hear him and Vesuvia drop down to the next level. She had to make a decision. The lead snowman tensed up. Its orange missile nose rocketed out of its face, on a heat-seeking course for Evie. She looked helplessly at the old prisoner, then dove for the hole in the floor, crying, "I'm sorry. I'm so sorry!"

She slipped through just before the carrot collided with the ground and exploded, sealing up the hole.

Evie landed hard on her rump, on another icy floor. It was so dark, Evie couldn't see where her brother and her nemesis had landed.

Somewhere across the room, Vesuvia apparently had similar issues. "Where *are* we? Turn on the lights."

Evie felt around, her hands stretched out in front of her. She settled on something cold and metal. It was round, like a big beach ball, and there was another, smaller metal ball resting on top of it.

"What is this place?" Rick whispered.

"Why are you whispering?" Vesuvia demanded. "Will someone turn the lights on? Turn—on—the—lights!"

Someone did. Pairs of little red lights, no bigger than lumps of coal, winked on. Hundreds of them. More turned on by the second.

"Uh, guys," Evie stammered. Two red lights had appeared directly in front of her. But these weren't just ordinary lights—they were eyes. And they were built into the object she'd been touching.

"Snowmen robots!" Vesuvia screamed. "Rick, you've gotta get us out of here!"

Rick switched on his thermal torch and heated the floor.

The snowmen came closer. Evie backed away, thrusting her torch at them. She circled Rick and Vesuvia, trying to keep the robots at bay.

Evie begged, "Hurry, Rick. You have to hurry!"

The snowmen recoiled when Evie aimed her torch at

them, but she couldn't point it at all of them at once.

"I'm almost through."

"Almost isn't fast enough!" Vesuvia wailed. "I'm too beautiful to die!" A snowman clamped a spindly hand on her shoulder. "Aieeee!"

One of the snowmen grabbed for Evie. She swatted it with her torch. The snowman fell back, knocking over the others behind him.

"I'm through!" Rick shouted. A cone of white light appeared from the hole in the floor.

Vesuvia didn't need telling twice. She jumped in.

"Evie, come on!" Rick called.

A snowman grabbed Evie's torch. She struggled for it, unable to break free.

"Just leave it!" Rick yelled.

She released the torch and slid into the hole after her brother, landing in a brightly lit hallway. But they weren't safe yet.

Vesuvia shook her head. "It seems that your genius getaway plan is off to yet another great start. Look!"

The Polar Bear stood at the far end growling at them. "You are only making things harder for yourselves. The time it takes to apprehend you is directly proportionate to the time you spend frozen here. Oh well, works for me." He dropped to all fours, roared, and charged the kids.

Evie ran, Rick and Vesuvia racing alongside her. Rick pointed at a set of double doors. "In here!" They made a sharp left and pushed through the doors. Another stairwell.

The Polar Bear crashed into the open doors, ripping them off their frames.

"Man, that guy has a thing against doors," Evie joked as the kids hurried down the stairs.

Clang! Bang! The sound of the Polar Bear thumping his metal-encased chest echoed in Evie's ears as she took the steps three at a time. The cyborg warden crouched, turning his body into a wrecking ball. He tipped forward and tumbled down the steps, only turning when he smashed into a wall.

Vesuvia sighed. "This dude doesn't give up!"

He chased them deep into the prison, down flight after flight. The stairs ended in a small room with a single door, marked "EMERGENCY EXIT." Evie could feel the Polar Bear right behind them. Without hesitation she opened the door.

"We're almost there!" she exclaimed. At the far end of the next room was a tunnel that led to the outside of the iceberg prison. Evie could see the overcast sky peeking through.

"Yeah, but first we have to get across that giant chasm." Rick pointed out.

"Wait, what?! Did you just say *giant chasm*?" Vesuvia barged to the front, pushing Evie out of the way. Between them and the tunnel was a narrow catwalk that stretched over the chasm in question. Somewhere below, the ocean roared.

"Yeah, uh, that's a giant chasm."

"It's either this or be Polar Bear food." Evie said. Then

she hurried across the catwalk, resuming her spot at the front. Vesuvia was right behind her, shoving her in the back and urging her along. Rick took up the rear.

The Polar Bear barged into the room. He pounced forward, landing hard on the catwalk with a tremendous *CRACK!*

"Go! Go!" Rick shouted. Evie reached the far side. She was almost knocked down as Vesuvia pushed past her. Then the catwalk broke.

"The destruction of Winterpole property will result in a longer SENTEEEENNNNCE!" the Polar Bear roared as he tumbled into the pit. His voice faded as he vanished.

Rick ran. Evie screamed his name as he sprinted across the falling catwalk. At the last second he leaped. The catwalk fell into oblivion. He wasn't going to make it. Evie held out her hands. Rick grabbed her before slamming into the ledge. He dangled over the pit, his feet scraping the smooth wall. Evie's grip was slipping.

Vesuvia stood at the entrance to the tunnel, so close to the exit, and freedom. Evie turned to her, desperately. "Vesuvia! Help! Please, help me!" She couldn't hold on to Rick forever. But she could see that look in Vesuvia's eyes. That look of victory, of getting what she wanted. Vesuvia knew all she had to do to escape the Prison at the Pole was to leave the Lanes behind. Let them suffer whatever fate Winterpole could cook up.

But then Vesuvia did something surprising. She ran back to the edge of the cliff, reached down, and grabbed one of Rick's arms. Grunting with exertion, the two girls pulled Rick to safety.

Evie couldn't believe it—Vesuvia had actually come back to help! Evie had never seen Vesuvia do anything for someone other than herself. Maybe Grandma Condolini was right. Prison had changed Vesuvia. Maybe there *was* good in her.

Vesuvia glared at them. "Well, quit staring at me, Lames. Grandma's waiting."

Evie, Rick, and Vesuvia ran through the tunnel and emerged from the frigid iceberg. They paddled out to sea, all three taking turns rowing. It didn't take long before they were far enough away from the Prison at the Pole for Sprout to land the *Roost* in the water and scoop them up.

Inside, Sprout was waiting for them, cowboy hat in his hands. He nodded at Vesuvia when she appeared. "Well, howdy, ma'am. Awful nice to put a face to the name I've heard so much about."

Vesuvia shoved Sprout into the wall as she walked past. "Out of my way, you hillbilly! I've been frozen in a block of ice for six weeks. There's no way I'm going to spend my first moments of freedom talking to you three."

Evie shook her head. It looked like Vesuvia hadn't changed at all.

A FEW HOURS AFTER THE DARING ESCAPE FROM THE PRISON AT THE POLE, THE *ROOST* WAS coming up on New Boca. At the rear of the bridge, Vesuvia sat on a wooden bench, acting like she owned the place. They had offered her clean, dry clothes, but Vesuvia refused, claiming that she was "appalled" by their fashion sense. She settled for one of Mom's bathrobes, which pooled around her feet.

Evie, meanwhile, sat on the floor in front of Vesuvia and didn't take her eyes off their new guest for one minute.

Vesuvia glared. "What are you looking at, Peevy Evie?"

"Just the person who sent robots to attack our continent." Evie glared right back.

Rick didn't know how to feel. He kept trying to tell himself they had freed Vesuvia because they needed to; otherwise they couldn't root the eighth continent. But she had saved his life seemingly without ulterior motive. It was all too strange to process.

"I can't believe none of y'all didn't get blown up by

them snow guards and their nose missiles! A carrot as a weapon. What a great idea!" Sprout grabbed his nose and pulled it, making machine gun sounds.

Rick had told Sprout all about their wild race through the prison.

"Y'all should have a security system like that on the eighth continent."

"We will," Rick said. "It'll be designed by the oversight committee. I'm thinking automated hoverships."

"Don't listen to him, Sprout," Evie said as she swiveled in her chair, even though no one had asked her opinion. "There will be a volunteer security force on the eighth continent. But crime won't be an issue, because it'll be a utopia."

Rick smiled at Sprout. "As you can see, there is still so much Evie doesn't understand."

"I understand you've got a meatball for a head!" Evie snapped.

"Ooooh!" Vesuvia purred from her seat. "Looks like there's trouble in non-Miami paradise."

Rick didn't want to show Vesuvia any more weakness than he and Evie already had. Even if Vesuvia *had* saved him, she had a history of exploiting such facts to her advantage. Not long ago it had nearly cost him the eighth continent.

"Hey, look." Sprout pointed. "There's New Boca straight ahead."

They landed the *Roost* beside Grandma Condolini's inflatable water castle. Vesuvia clapped her hands when she saw it. "Ooooh! This is so exactly like Granny. Whee!"

Two of the pink robo-gorillas escorted the children into the castle. They boarded inflatable boats and were sent on the twisting journey through the castle's flooded tunnels. The Big Game Huntress met them in the throne room, where 2-Tor lay sprawled out on plastic pillows, his worm-bloated stomach puffed out like a balloon.

Vesuvia leaped from her boat, bounced nimbly across the springy floor, and landed in Grandma Condolini's lap. The old lady's drink fell from her hand, sinking to the bottom of the pool. The inflatable flamingo's neck flopped wildly at the additional weight of the girl.

"Susu! My darling precious girl. What have those bureaucratic bozos done to you? You're so skinny!"

"Oh, Granny, it was terrible. I ate nothing but snow the whole time, and there wasn't a hot tub in sight."

"You poor thing! Elizabeth, run-don't-walk to the kitchen. This pretty princess needs a pink pineapple smoothie and a spa treatment. Make it snappy!"

The Big Game Huntress toddled off, snarling like one of the animals she hunted. Vesuvia squeezed her grandmother tightly and purred, "You remembered my favorite smoothie! I missed you so much, Granny."

"There, there, Susu. You're home, now. You never need to worry again."

Rick watched this scene with impatience and mild disgust. It was clear that no matter how long he stood there with Evie and Sprout at his side, the royal family of Condo Corp was not going to interrupt their reunion to notice them. "Pardon me, but we have returned your granddaughter to you safely, as you requested. I believe it is time for you to uphold your end of the—"

"—Bargain? I believe you're right." Grandma Condolini took out a handheld fan and stuck it in the water. The spinning blades acted like a propeller, pushing her and Vesuvia to the shore. "Will some young gentleman help me out of this flamingo, or does an old lady have to do everything herself?"

While Rick stood mouth agape, Sprout swooped in. He held out both hands, allowing Grandma Condolini and Vesuvia to step onto dry ground. "Ooooh!" Vesuvia said. "So strong!"

Rick could hear Evie gritting her teeth.

"Yes, he is quite the gentleman." Grandma Condolini patted Sprout on the back. "So, you know where this super root of yours is, yes? You know how to get there?"

"I know where it is, ma'am," Sprout said.

"Excellent. I've notified my employees that you will be passing through. I appreciate all you have done for my family. Please enjoy your super root."

Rick bowed his head. "Thank you, Ms. Condolini."

She nudged Vesuvia. "There, you see that, Susu? Manners. Even a Lane can learn. Now children, shoo-shoo! Go find your root."

Vesuvia felt so good to be free. It felt giant-slice-of-bubblegum-birthday-cake good. It felt bathing-in-a-hot-tub-of-her-enemies'-tears good.

It felt having-your-own-continent good.

The muscles in her cheeks were contorted in a fake smile so painful it hurt her brain. She waved, watching those idiots Rick and Evie, their dirty talking bird, and their ugly redneck friend leave.

When they were gone, Vesuvia gave Granny a look of great offense. "How could you help them, you crazy old leather purse? They're the enemy! Ugh. I feel disgusting just thinking about it."

While Vesuvia ranted, her grandmother's smile widened, her dentures gleaming. All at once, Granny burst out laughing.

Vesuvia scowled. "What are you cackling about?"

Granny pulled Vesuvia into a tight hug. "Oh my darling girl, I missed you so. When those fools showed up, I just knew it meant I would see you again. But do you thank your granny for sending them to rescue you? Nope, not even a word. That Piffle man spoiled you so." Granny pulled back. "Of course, none of this would have even been an issue if you hadn't gotten yourself caught like an idiot."

"I'm so sorry, Granny. I didn't mean it. I was trying to get us a whole new continent to build condos on. Think of the profit!"

"Yes, yes, I know. I'm sure your heart was in the right place. But you have to be careful."

Vesuvia nodded. "I know. So what's next?"

"Next? That's easy. Next we are going to take the eighth continent for ourselves."

18

THE JUNGLE WAS SO HUMID EVIE COULD BARELY BREATHE. TRAVELING TO THE RAINFOREST, THEN the Arctic, then back to the rainforest again, she was getting climatological whiplash!

Sprout, quite at home in the sweltering heat, barely perspired at all. He hacked at the plants with his weathered machete, clearing a path. 2-Tor chugged along behind him, his feathers damp with sweat. Rick took up the rear, gasping for air. His glasses were all fogged up.

"Do you think we did the right thing?" Rick asked Evie breathlessly as they walked.

It gave her comfort to know she wasn't the only one who had doubts about returning Vesuvia to her grandmother. "I don't know. I feel like we took a big risk rescuing her."

Rick nodded. "Dad always says that risk-taking is good, but you have to be prepared to deal with the consequences."

Evie had been trying to remain focused on the mission. According to the continental collision clock, they only had until sundown to stop the crash. "As long as we save the eighth continent and Australia, that's all that matters."

They came upon a giant leaf that hung over an arch of branches. Sprout pushed it aside like a thick green curtain. The glade of super root lay beyond.

The sun shone brightly in this circular clearing. The grass was tall, and at the center was a vine-covered boulder beside a calm pool. The children raced to the center of the glade shouting, "Is that it? Wahoo! We did it!" And 2-Tor took flight, caught up in the thrill of the moment.

Evie was the first to reach the boulder. She inspected the vines, checking to see if any resembled the super root Professor Doran had given them.

"Hey y'all, check this out over here!" Sprout delicately pulled a plant away from the boulder. The black bulbs of the super root were tucked in a bud where the petiole of a leaf met the vine.

"It's funny these guys can root a continent—they're so little!" Evie observed.

"Yes," Sprout said. "Boy, do they ever grow big. Sometimes I call it the upstairs-downstairs vine, because there's always so much going on with it upstairs with the plant and downstairs with the root." Sprout gently pet the top of the plant like it was a small, furry animal. "Whole trees have been known to sprout from a super root, covering wide areas. It's sort of like the Pando quaking aspen grove, in Utah."

2-Tor squawked. "Oh yes! My memory banks contain data on that forest. Or rather, I *remember* learning about that forest. Fascinating. You see, the entire forest of quaking aspen is actually a single living organism."

"Wow, that's pretty cool!" Rick said, sounding amazed.

Sprout plucked one of the bulbs from the plant and stuck it in a little plastic baggy, which he then tucked into the breast pocket of his shirt. "There," he said. "Now what?"

"Now back to the eighth continent!" Evie declared.

Rick nodded and adopted a somber tone. "That's right. This mission isn't over yet."

On the trip back to the *Roost*, a strange odor filled Evie's nose.

"What is that, smoke?" Evie sniffed.

"Smells like a campfire," Sprout said.

Rick squinted to see between the trees. "It's no campfire. Look!"

A fire had broken out in New Boca, and the flames were spreading through the area. The fire leaped from trendy boutique to palm tree to rascal-scooter surplus store.

"Oh dear me!" 2-Tor gasped. "What a terrible accident."

"That's no accident, 2-Tor," Rick said. "We were just here a few minutes ago. The fire spread too far too quickly for it to have occurred by sheer happenstance."

"Are you saying someone set this fire on purpose?" asked Evie.

"That's exactly what I'm saying."

"Outta the way, squirts!" someone yelled over the sound of a siren. "The Old Bat Bucket Brigade is *on the job*!"

The group jumped to the side as two long fire trucks

The group jumped to the side as two long fire trucks zoomed by. Grandmothers hung from the sides of the trucks, armed with hoses and hatchets. They began blasting the flames with high-pressure water, but they couldn't hold back the fire's advance. The grannies were outmatched.

Soon the fire spread to the ring of trees around New Boca. Sprout stared in dismay at the burning forest. "Who would ever set fire to—oh . . ."

Above the town rose an immense inflatable blimp shaped like a blue whale. Only it wasn't blue.

It was pink.

A loudspeaker crackled, the sound echoing from the flying whale above them. "Attention ugly losers, this is your Chief Executive Officer Vesuvia Piffle coming to you live from the Condo Corp flagship *Big Whale*. You've done such good work for Condo Corp, but I'm afraid that our partnership must be cut short. Me and Granny have important business to attend to at the eighth continent, so we're going to have to let you go. That means you're going to be *terminated*. In other words, YOU'RE FIRED!" Her maniacal laughter echoed off the trees.

Grandma Condolini cut over the speaker. "Give it a rest, Susu."

"Yes, Granny."

The *Big Whale* gained height and drifted away. "Well, you can't say that Grandma Condolini didn't keep her word," Evie said once the vast ship had disappeared from view.

"How do you figure?" Rick asked.

"She gave us the super root. She just neglected to mention that she'd make sure we all died in a fire."

"Nice, Evie." Rick looked ahead. The fire was almost upon them. "We have to get to the *Roost*," he said.

"Wait." Sprout grabbed them. "The forest around the town is like a fireworks factory. It'll keep burning until there's nothing left. We can't just leave. We have to stop the fire somehow."

2-Tor straightened. "Harsh though it may seem, I cannot advise you children to take unnecessary risks. We have the super root. We should depart immediately and make haste for the eighth continent."

The fire had consumed the buildings around them and was closing in. It was getting hot. Very hot. Soon there would be nothing left of the Lane kids, New Boca, or the whole rainforest.

"I dunno, 2-Tor," Rick said. "What about the jungle?"

"What about Australia?" 2-Tor clacked his beak anxiously.

Rick wiped the sweat off his brow. The jungle heat really was intense. "I know, 2-Tor. We're short on time. But we can't just leave this mess."

Sprout's eyes glimmered with hope.

Evie nodded in agreement with her brother. "Follow me," she said. "I have an idea."

Like maniacs, they rushed through the town, dancing around burning carts selling reed hats and cough drops. Evie was careful not to touch anything. She covered her nose and mouth with her shirt, so she wouldn't accidentally inhale too much smoke. Soon they reached Grandma Condolini's inflatable castle. The fire burned all around them, darkening the sky.

"Uh, Evie, what are we doing here?" Rick looked up at the wobbling castle.

"Grandma Condolini's castle is inflated like a balloon, but inside there are lakes and streams. So really it's like a water balloon. And what happens when you pop a water balloon?"

"You get wet. So that means . . ."

Sprout nearly jumped out of his spurs. "That means we can use it to hit New Boca in the face!"

"Exactly!" Evie smiled. "Sprout, give me your machete."

He handed it over. She plunged the blade into the castle's exterior wall.

It didn't work. The machete pushed a divot into the plastic without tearing through. Then the wall sprung back into place, knocking Evie to the ground. The machete landed in the earth beside her.

"It's like poking a pillow," Evie said, righting herself.

Sprout pulled his machete free and helped Evie up. "Let's try together."

The fire was close now, very close. Evie coughed violently as they slashed at the thick plastic.

"Keep going!" Rick urged. "I think it's starting to work!"

They had carved a shallow groove into the thick material when behind them a voice cried, "Lanes! Don't move!"

Evie winced. Sprout kept sawing away while the others turned. The Big Game Huntress emerged from the fire, the singed edges of her animal skins glowing. She held her bowzooka over her shoulder, ready to fire.

Pointing at 2-Tor, the Big Game Huntress said, "The old hag ditched me! But I'm not leaving this mess empty-handed. I'm taking that crow. Now give him to me."

"You're making a big mistake," Evie warned.

"Are you threatening me? Listen, little girl, I fought a pack of hyenas bare-handed when you weren't even in your parents' imagination. Now step aside, and give me that bird."

Sprout was still cutting through the plastic. He was deeper, but he needed another minute.

"Leave me be, vile poacher!" 2-Tor pointed a feather at her. "I am not some quarry to be stuffed and mounted."

"That's exactly what you are, bird," the Big Game Huntress said. "Either you come with me and become my trophy later, or fight and I'll make you fried chicken right now." The light of the looming flames gave her face a demonic tinge.

"I refuse to obey someone so merciless," 2-Tor said.

"So be it. I gave you a choice." She took aim with her bowzooka.

Just before she pulled the trigger, Sprout sliced through the plastic wall of the castle. It split like a ripe tomato, and a gush of water lashed the air, striking the Big Game Huntress firmly in the chest. She screamed as the blast knocked her back behind the wall of fire.

The cut in the side of the castle ripped open and water fell out in a great torrent. The outpour flowed across the landscape, swallowing the fire and tossing the inflatable animal boats in every direction.

Evie struggled to grab on to something but the current was too strong. It scooped her up and carried her down the main boulevard, doing the same to Sprout, Rick, and 2-Tor.

The castle buckled, collapsing in a dripping heap of mangled plastic. "Oof," Evie grunted as the unexpected water ride dropped her in a big puddle of mud just beyond the wreckage of the deflated castle.

The golfers Herb and Scotty surfed past her, clinging to their golf bags. Herb waved. "Hello, Miss! Thank you for saving the town."

"Hah?" Scotty clutched his friend. "Don't worry, Herb. I won't let you drown." The old men floated away.

Evie pulled free of the mud and splashed back to the *Roost*. The others had just arrived and were standing in front of the hovership, soaking wet, but grinning.

"We did it!" Sprout said. "We doused that fire all right. Now the only question is where that awful Big Game Huntress is at."

2-Tor coughed uncomfortably. "As we've already obtained the super root, I suggest that we not dawdle here trying to find out. Shall we depart?"

"An excellent recommendation, 2-Tor." Evie flung her arms around him as they hurried aboard the *Roost*.

LONG BEFORE VESUVIA WAS BORN, CONDO CORP HAD INVESTED IN THE FUTURE OF LUXURY transport, purchasing a fleet of cruise ships, airplanes, Segways, and blimps to provide the world's most expensive travel for the rich and famous. The crown jewel of the Condo Corp armada was the *Big Whale*, Grandma Condolini's personal airship.

Vesuvia delighted in lounging on the bridge of the *Big Whale*. The best part was the pamper-bots who were on hand, quite literally, to attend to Vesuvia's manicure needs.

And thank goodness. After six weeks frozen in a wall, her fingernails were ghastly.

Granny, for her part, clearly had no time to worry about a manicure—and not just because her nails were already polished to perfection. She sat on a stool at the front of the bridge, flying the enormous blimp to the eighth continent. Unfortunately, the stool did little to help with Granny's height issue. Even with it, she was so short she could barely see over the steering wheel.

Vesuvia stretched like a lazy kitten and sighed, taking in the euphoria-inducing plastic smell of the inflatable couches around her. "Oh, Granny, it feels *so good* to be out of that frozen dump. And now the Lanes are cooked. This has been the most loveliest day of the year."

"Oh you think so, huh? Ha! Double ha!" Granny made a face like she was sucking on a grapefruit. "While you've been on your ski trip, the rest of us have been working."

"Ski trip!? You think that icy pit was a vacation? I'm lucky I escaped alive!"

"You're lucky *I* sent those stupid brats to break you out, or you'd still be there, whining and doing no one any good I'm sure."

Vesuvia pulled away from the pamper-bot, who blatted disapprovingly. She stomped over to the pilot's seat and stuck a half-painted finger in Granny's face. "But now I'm out, and I'm ready to take my continent, so stop holding me accountable for things I did in the past. That's not fair!"

Granny sniffed. "Your petulance serves you well, child. It's an admirable quality for a CEO to possess. Let me tell you what I've been up to during your unfortunate absence."

"Yes, please!"

"Well," Granny said, "I wasn't about to let those stupid Lanes get away with locking up my precious Susu. As soon as I heard what happened at the eighth continent, I sent the Piffle Pink Patrol to smash them good!"

There was nothing Vesuvia had missed more while she had been locked up than her beloved Piffle Pink Patrol. Not even smoothies or the blueprints to New Miami. The PPP was her special army of plastic robot animals. There was Stuffings, the Bird Brigade, and of course, her dearest fishy companion, the robo-shark Chompedo. If anyone was capable of smashing the Lanes, it was them.

Granny went on. "But our pink robots ran into a problem when those lousy Lanes hit them with an EMP. The robots were heavily damaged and crashed into the eighth continent, knocking it off course."

Vesuvia threw her hands in the air. "Oh! So that's why Evie Lane was all up in my grille about the Piffle Pink Patrol attacking her stupid continent. She blamed me. But *you* were the one who sent them. Classy move, Granny. Very classy!"

"What no one knew," Granny smiled, "was that I had intended for this to happen all along. With the continent destabilized, its occupants would scatter to find a solution. Now there are no Lanes left on the eighth continent."

"Right," Vesuvia said. "But the Lanes said Winterpole has an outpost there now."

"What?! Those bureaucratic bozos? My intel didn't tell me anything about that."

"Your intel must stink worse than your dentures," Vesuvia sneered.

Granny swatted her. Fortunately, Vesuvia's plastic hairspray-coated 'do cushioned the blow.

"I may have a solution to the Winterpole problem," Vesuvia said. "I need to make a call."

Vesuvia left the bridge and wandered through the *Big*

Whale, looking for a quiet place to use her phone. She walked past the kitchens, where chef-bots were furiously chopping fruit to be made into smoothies, and past one of the blimp's three heated swimming pools, where a bunch of inflatable animals floated on the surface. When she reached the giant wardrobe that took up the majority of the blimp's center, she had to force herself not to get distracted by all the fancy clothes. She had a mission to accomplish, after all.

Finally, Vesuvia reached the back of the ship. Winded from her journey, she plopped down on an inflatable stool and took out the new phone Granny had given her as a welcome-home present. Then she dialed the only number she knew by heart.

The phone rang. And rang again. At long last a voice was audible on the other end of the line. "Hello?" it asked. The voice was meek and quiet, like a mouse. But it was the only voice Vesuvia wanted to hear, that of her ex-but-maybe-not-ex-best-friend.

"Diana?" Vesuvia asked. "Diana is that you? Tell me what you're doing right this instant."

"What am I . . . ? I'm . . . processing permission slips at my internship. Who is this? Vesuvia?"

"Yes, Diana, it is me, the best thing that ever happened to you. And aren't you lucky that I'm calling you now? Don't answer yet. I have some good news. Even though you betrayed me for no good reason and all that, I'm willing to let bygones be bygones unless you make me mad again. And you know what that means? It means I want you to come back to work for me. Isn't that fantastic?"

Diana's voice came back quiet and fearful. "Vesuvia, um . . . I don't want to work for you anymore. I have a job. And you're in prison."

"Oh, Diana, ignorant as usual. I'm not in prison. I'm free! I broke out. And now I'm going to take over the eighth continent with your help."

"What? Vesuvia"—Diana lowered her voice—"I could get in a lot of trouble just for having this conversation. I don't want to help you. Don't call me again."

"I think we'd start by destroying the base Winterpole has set up on the continent," Vesuvia said thoughtfully. "Your knowledge of their tactics will be essential. Do you think you could get your mother to betray Winterpole for us? You're going to have to ask her about that right away."

There was a long pause. This was not cool. When Vesuvia gave her best friend an order, she expected an immediate "Yes, Vesuvia," or "Anything you wish, Vesuvia." And she usually got one.

"Hello?" Vesuvia asked the phone in a tone that usually belonged to Diana.

No reply.

"Diana?"

The voice that returned to Vesuvia was not Diana's. "Beeee boooo bEEEEEE. Please hang up and try your call again. If you need assistance, dial an operator."

It was hard for Vesuvia to process what had just happened. Diana had never told her *no* before. It had never occurred to Vesuvia that there would come a time when Diana didn't want to be around her and help her solve her problems. That was what Diana always did. The truth was, Diana was the only person Vesuvia really liked having around. Obviously Vesuvia was doing her a big favor by hanging out with someone so much less popular and attractive than she was. But now that Diana was gone . . . was it possible Diana had also been doing Vesuvia a favor . . . by being her friend?

Vesuvia definitely did not like the feeling inside her at the moment, and it was not going away. She wanted to blame Diana for feeling horrible, but she couldn't. It was a strange sensation and it freaked her out.

Back on the bridge, Vesuvia told Granny about the setback.

"So you're telling me you don't have a way to get rid of the Winterpole outpost?" Granny snorted loudly. "And you also feel bad? What does that even mean?"

"I don't know. . . ." Vesuvia thought about it. "It's like I have a weight on my chest. I want to lie down and don't want to stand up."

Granny scoffed. "What you're feeling is *sadness*, my dear. I can't say I'm surprised you've never experienced it before. Condolini women are known for being *fabulous* so much of the time, even those of us who are half-Piffle."

"What can I do?" Vesuvia asked, worried this sadness would damage her reputation as a Condolini woman.

"It just so happens that I have the perfect thing to solve both our problems. We need to get supplies to wipe out that Winterpole outpost, and we need to make you feel better. So that leaves just one option. Susu, my dear, we are going shopping!"

20

BACK ON THE *ROOST*, RICK KNEW WHAT THEY HAD TO DO NEXT. "WE NEED TO RESCUE MOM."

"WHAT!?!" Evie exclaimed, pushing back from the table of maps they'd all been scouring over. "We haven't rooted the eighth continent yet and you just told us that it's going to collide with Australia in a few hours."

2-Tor squawked. "I must say, Richard, it does indeed seem very foolhardy to interrupt the mission."

Sprout listened, looking agreeable, but the puzzled look on his face made it obvious he was as baffled as the others.

Rick ripped off his glasses and polished the lenses on his shirt. He was already losing the crowd. "People, please! We have to stay focused. Look. We can't take on Winterpole and Condo Corp by ourselves. We need help, but we don't even know where Dad is."

"I dunno, Rick. We made it this far by ourselves. Why do you think we suddenly need Mom to come to the rescue?"

"Because before we didn't have Vesuvia in our hair. Face it. We messed up letting Grandma Condolini trick us.

It's clear we can't do this on our own. I feel like we're back where we started. Winterpole and Vesuvia and us all racing to control the eighth continent, and we're in last place."

"I was against freeing Vesuvia from the start," Evie pointed out.

Sprout put up his hands. "Look y'all, there's no need to point fingers. That doesn't do anyone any good."

"It would have done us plenty of good if we hadn't broken that evil, vile villain out of her cell."

2-Tor squawked. "I must say, Richard, even I was quite surprised to see you take on such an abhorrent task."

"Well, I didn't see you protest when you were stuffing your face with Grandma Condolini's earthworm salad."

"Oh my. How rude!" 2-Tor turned up his beak in offense.

"I think we should change course for the stain in the South Pacific, find out from the Cleanaspot people there where Mom is being held, and bust her out of wherever it is. Once Mom is free, she can help us rally the ships and workers of Cleanaspot to stand a decent chance against Vesuvia and Condo Corp."

"In a perfect world that plan sounds fine, but the stain is so out of the way. We don't have time to make detours, Rick."

Rick pointed at the maps on the table. "I've thought carefully about this decision, Evie. I've considered our options. The stain is due south from our current position. The continent is far to the west, only a few hundred miles from Australia. Yes, it's out of the way. Yes, it'll delay our return to the eighth continent. But through my analysis, I have determined that this is our best hope. You should trust me."

Snorting loudly, Evie said, "You mean the way we should trust the scientist dictators you want running the eighth continent? Good thing we're not under your rule, and this, this right here"—she pointed between herself, 2-Tor, and Sprout—"this is a democracy."

2-Tor blinked awkwardly. "Your knowledge of my old personality circuits is sound. It would be my preference, of course, to reunite with Mrs. Lane."

Rick let out a sigh of relief. At least someone was on his side. "Thank you, 2-Tor."

"On the other wing," 2-Tor went on, "I do see the merits in both arguments. It is only fitting in this case that I abstain from the vote."

"No, 2-Tor!" Rick pleaded desperately. "You're one of us. You're not even a robot any more. Of course you should vote. Vote your conscience."

"I must not," said 2-Tor.

Rick turned to Sprout, who had been listening thoughtfully. "Fine, then Sprout, you're the deciding vote. What are we going to do? Rush into danger unprepared, or go get backup?"

Sprout tipped back his hat and wiped his brow with a handkerchief. "Well, shucks, Rick, I've been thinking real hard about this here argument. I always heard you want someone sitting shotgun when you ride into danger."

"Yes, exactly!" Rick said. "Someone at your side."

Evie tugged on his arm. "But Sprout, we don't have time. Besides, you came all this way to see the super root in action. You'll miss it if you're at the stain. Because I'm taking the *Roost* to the eighth continent now, no matter what Rick says."

"You can't do that," Rick said.

"Watch me," Evie said defiantly. "Look, I want to rescue Mom too, but we don't have time right now. If you absolutely *have* to free her right this second, take an escape pod and go find her. Meanwhile, I'll be saving the continent from our enemies and saving Australia from the continent."

"You never listen and you never think, Evie! Even Vesuvia would be a better sister than you." Rick felt how cruel this was even as he was saying it. But he was so mad at her he could barely see straight.

Evie stuck her tongue out at him. "I'm not the one screaming and bossing everyone around. Say goodbye, Sprout. Rick is leaving."

"Don't be ridiculous," Rick said. "Sprout is coming with me. He's my friend, not yours. Come on, Sprout. Let's go."

Sprout stood still, hat in hand, looking awkward. "Aw, shucks, Rick. Don't make me choose. Evie's right. I sure do want to see the super root in action."

Rick watched helplessly as Sprout followed Evie to the bridge. How had he lost that argument? He had spent so much time analyzing the different possible outcomes and sculpting his replies to each branch in the dialogue tree.

2-Tor placed a warm wing on his shoulder. "There,

there, Richard. It is all right. I will accompany you to your mother." The bird's company did little to comfort Rick as he strapped into the acorn escape pod. "Detach docking cable!" 2-Tor said, throwing a lever.

With a snap, the escape pod broke free and rocketed across the ocean in the opposite direction of where the *Roost* was heading. Rick watched his beloved hovership fade into the distance, feeling as disconnected from his life as the continent was from the ocean floor.

SO THAT'S HOW THEY ESCAPED, DIANA THOUGHT, STARING AT THE HOLE THAT THE LANES AND Vesuvia had carved through at least a dozen prison floors. Leaning against the Vesuvia-size divot in the icy wall, she watched the adults argue. The warden, known as the Polar Bear, was in hot water.

Literally.

During his chase with the Lanes and the "Piffle fugitive," as Mister Snow called Vesuvia, the Polar Bear had fallen into a pit, struck a steam pipe, and superheated the base of the prison, melting it. Diana had never heard of someone making an iceberg sink, but from the looks on her mother's and Mister Snow's faces, they did not appreciate their iceberg being the first to do so.

"They navigated the prison too easily," the Polar Bear blubbered. "It must have been an inside job."

Mrs. Maple rolled her eyes. "You're making excuses for your incompetence, warden. *You* are the one with all the access codes. If anyone from Winterpole helped the Piffle fugitive escape, it was probably you."

"Me!? No, no. I love Winterpole. Why else would I be freezing my paws off in this awful place?"

Diana's mother gasped in offense. This was not going to be good.

Mister Snow drew a piece of cyber paper and snapped it. An electrical charge shot from the paper and struck the Polar Bear. He immediately dropped to the floor, writhing in agony.

"Article Three, Subsection Eight—Winterpole facilities are to be spoken of with respect and mild reverence," Mister Snow sneered.

"I'm sorry!" the Polar Bear choked. "Please stop!" Diana grimaced as Mister Snow put the paper away. Across the room, Benjamin Nagg, the only other trainee to come with the agents on this mission, smirked knowingly.

"Hey Mister Snow," Benjamin said, "permission to make an observation, sir?"

"Granted, trainee."

"Maybe this fat old man is right. After all, one of Piffle's known accomplices works at Winterpole. In fact, she's here right now."

Diana glared. "I know what you're insinuating, Benjamin, and it's utterly ridiculous. I'm the one who testified against Vesuvia in the first place. I helped Mister Snow find her after the Battle of the Garbage Patch. Tell him, Mister Snow. Tell this sower of discord that his suggestion is absurd. I should throw a dozen demerits at him for slander."

Despite Diana's lashing, Benjamin went right on grinning. Mister Snow's eyes grew as he stared at Diana. "The trainee has a point, Miss Maple. There is evidence you helped the Piffle fugitive out of jams on many occasions. Have you had any contact with her since her detention?"

"Have I . . . um . . ." Diana tried to summon the words. She'd had nothing to do with the prison break, but she *had* received an unprompted phone call from Vesuvia just before leaving for the Pole.

Diana wanted nothing to do with Vesuvia and had told her as much. But she didn't want to lie. Turning to her mother, Diana said, "Mom, tell them to leave me alone. This is crazy."

Her mother's voice was cold. "I don't know, Diana. They have a point. *Have* you had any contact with Vesuvia? I suggest you answer my colleagues."

"I won't dignify these questions with a response!" Diana shouted. She'd heard someone yell that on a TV legal drama, and figured it was the correct thing to say.

Benjamin shivered with delight. "Uhhuhhuh. Mister Snow, we have a hostile suspect. Might I recommend enhanced interrogation techniques?"

"She looks pretty guilty to me!" The Polar Bear looked away and wiped his mouth, obviously happy not to be the center of attention anymore.

Diana's eyes darted between her mother, Mister Snow, and Benjamin, her panic growing. They stepped closer. "Have you had any contact with the fugitive?" asked Benjamin.

"Did you help her escape?" asked Mister Snow.

Her mother put a hand on her shoulder. It wasn't meant to be comforting. "Where is Vesuvia now?"

"I don't know!" Diana screamed, pushing away from them. "I didn't help her escape."

Mister Snow and her mother exchanged a look. Mrs. Maple nodded. "Very well, Diana. We believe you. Now, let us return to Winterpole Headquarters. Polar Bear, you will continue your duties here as warden without pay until you receive the verdict of your disciplinary hearing. I give you my word that we will expedite the procedure. No one wishes to leave you in limbo."

"I appreciate that, ma'am," the Polar Bear said.

"Good. You should have the verdict in twelve to eighteen months."

"Months? Without pay?"

Diana's mother left the cell in a flurry. "Come along, Mister Snow. Trainees, we're going."

The others followed in Mrs. Maple's wake. The Polar Bear stayed behind, watching them go. He looked so miserable Diana couldn't help feeling bad for him, even if he had been terrible to her back in the cell.

As they walked the halls, headed to the landing pad on the roof, Benjamin stopped Diana, hissing like a snake. "Let's get one thing straight, Maple. I own you now. I've been monitoring your Winterpole communication line for weeks. I know you spoke to your old pal Vesuvia on the phone."

Diana shoved him hard with both hands. He snorted

in amusement. "I didn't help her escape!" she said. "I didn't want her to escape."

"Oh. Oh dear." For a second Benjamin looked regretful, but then his face morphed back into its sinister leer. "You must have me confused with someone who gives two ice cubes about *the truth*. I have evidence you spoke to her. That's all I need to convince everyone else here that you lied to superior Winterpole officers—and your own mother. As the daughter of the Secretary of Enforcement, you must know what the penalty is for *lying*."

"What do you care?"

"Care? Can't I want to defend the ideals of our noble organization? No, no. Of course that's silly. But you've had everything handed to you, and you don't deserve it. So now we both know who the better agent is. Cross me again, and you're finished."

He shoved her back, knocking her so hard in the chest that it dropped her to the cold floor. She clutched herself, gasping. Benjamin spun on his toes and hurried after the grown-up agents.

Diana's head was spinning. Benjamin could blab at any time, and then she'd be finished. Not just with Winterpole, but with her Mom too. She figured she might as well lock herself in one of these cells right now. She'd be back soon enough.

Looking up at the cell door in front of her, she saw the number. Z-99.

George Lane.

She crawled over to the door and pulled herself up. The small window in the door was blurry with frost. She breathed on the glass and wiped it clear.

The poor man was still in there, tied to the chair, fish falling on his head twice a minute. He looked as miserable as Diana felt. But there was nothing she could do for him.

Up on the landing pad, Mister Snow and Benjamin were already aboard their hovership. Diana's mother was waiting. "What took so long?"

"Nothing," Diana said. "Just had to catch my breath."

"We need to talk," her mother replied.

"Can we do it on the ship? I'm tired and it's freezing out here."

"No we cannot. Diana, you will not be returning to Geneva. You will be staying here."

"I told you I had nothing to do with Vesuvia's escape!"

Her mother shook her head. "This isn't about that. I'm . . . giving you a reward, for all your hard work. I need you to continue investigating the breakout. You can't do that if you're not at the Prison at the Pole. Get to the bottom of it. You can return to Winterpole once you've filed a full ten-thousand-page report."

"Ten thousand! By myself?"

"Some agents would be thankful to have their superior officer give them such an important assignment."

An important punishment is more like it, Diana thought. Her faith in Winterpole was unraveling at an alarming speed. The bureaucracy and the rules always took top billing, with only an occasional guest appearance by the ideals Diana held dear. Protect the environment, defend endangered animals, save the earth—Winterpole never *did* any of that stuff. Instead, they tracked down people who didn't get permission slips for arbitrary junk and slammed them with exorbitant penalties. Even their own agents weren't immune, as Diana had just discovered.

Making no effort to embrace her daughter, Mrs. Maple said, "Good luck with your mission. I look forward to your paperwork."

Diana was still standing on the landing pad, alone and in disbelief, when the hovership took off and flew home.

THE FIRST STOP ON GRANDMA CONDOLINI'S SHOPPING SPREE WAS TOTALLY SANE PETE'S USED Weapon Dealership—*Why Would You Think Pete Was Anything but Sane?*, a depot in Arizona for cannons, contraptions, and other calamitous inventions. Vesuvia had no interest in setting a dainty toe on the property, which featured not three, but four lawn flamingoes, and innumerable garden gnomes with hats in seven distinct colors. It was so tacky, Vesuvia nearly gagged.

Totally Sane Pete and several of his assistants emerged from the depot in Granny's wake. The old woman had a look of pure satisfaction on her face. Vesuvia could see why. The assistants each pushed large carts filled with hammer cannons, chainsaw launchers, and other destructive weapons.

"Back to the *Big Whale*, Susu! We're on to our next destination." Granny knew better than to waltz into Winterpole territory unprepared. That was a strategy guaranteed to land Vesuvia back at the Prison at the Pole. Instead, they flew around the globe, gathering tanks, attack robots, stylish boots, and other supplies from several of Granny's old friends—terrorists, warlords, military dictators, and an old crooner who stank of cigars and whose yellow teeth seemed to take up the entirety of his face.

It was oddly amusing to meet so many bizarre people, but this wasn't exactly the sort of shopping spree Vesuvia had in mind, so she was relieved when Granny said, "All right, I think we have everything. Now, to the eighth continent!"

Several hours later, Vesuvia and her grandmother had circled the globe. The eighth continent was at last visible through the front viewport of the *Big Whale*. Vesuvia bubbled with anticipation. She couldn't wait to make the continent her own.

Granny grabbed the megaphone she used to communicate with the crew and raised it to her lips. "Deploy the Piffle Pink Patrol!"

Pink robo-birds spilled from the hangar on the ship's underbelly. They looked pretty beat up from their last encounter with the Lanes, but Granny gave no sign to indicate she noticed or cared. "Excellent, excellent!" she cheered. "Good to see the patrol is operating at top efficiency."

Vesuvia mewed as she waved at the robots swooping past the window. "Pinky! Blinky! Peppercorn! Chompedo! Look at you fly!"

Granny barked into her megaphone. "Begin the bombardment!"

The Piffle Pink Patrol turned en masse and bombed the continent. Winterpole agents ran for cover. The robots pelted the ground with napalm, hydrochloric acid, and a mixture of orange juice and 2-percent milk.

"Milk?" Vesuvia asked.

"Not just regular milk, also chocolate milk. And strawberry for you, of course. Speaking of which"—Granny cranked up the volume on her megaphone—"WILL SOMEONE GET MY GRANDDAUGHTER SOME STRAWBERRY MILK!? Sigh. You see, Susu, the experimental bombardment is all part of my master plan."

"And what plan is that?" Vesuvia asked, accepting a glass of pink milk from a passing server-bot.

"Why, destroying the eighth continent, of course."

Vesuvia choked in response. Twin streams of strawberry milk shot from her nostrils. "Destroy it?! Have all those perms damaged your wrinkled old brain? What about New Miami?"

Granny clutched her chest wistfully. "Ah, to be young and narrow-minded again."

"*Excuse* me? Narrow-minded?"

"Don't be such a daft pineapple, Susu. There are more important things than New Miami."

"What did you just say?"

"Condo Corp has formed a partnership with another corporation to destroy the eighth continent and discover the chemical formula for the Eden Compound."

"Uh, good luck with that. Every last drop of that nasty

green Eden Compound was used to turn all the garbage into the land that now makes up the Lanes' precious continent. We lost most of the Condo Corp fleet, and it ruined my favorite jacket."

"I know," Granny said. "While you were having your holiday at Chez Winterpole, I was handling the insurance settlement. But think carefully now. The Eden Compound isn't really gone, it has merely changed, forming new earth with the old trash. Now, what if we could undo that transformation?"

"Then you'd have a bunch of yucky garbage again, and still no New Miami."

"You'd have a bunch of yucky garbage AND the Eden Compound. They would separate. And with the Eden Compound in hand, we could figure out how to make *more* Eden Compound. And then, with more Eden Compound, we could transform garbage dumps *anywhere in the world.*"

Vesuvia's head felt light, but maybe that was some of the strawberry milk sloshing around her skull. "You mean . . . two New Miamis?"

"Two *thousand* New Miamis! You see, we're destroying the eighth continent so we can profit off someone else's good idea later. In business we call that investing."

Two thousand New Miamis. Vesuvia's mind ran wild with the possibilities. Maybe she didn't need Diana after all. She could make the world she wanted all by herself, and no one could stop her, not even the stupid Lanes and their dumb bird. There was just one question.

"Granny, who did Condo Corp form their partnership with? Where'd you get this idea in the first place?"

Tapping her playfully on the nose, Granny said, "That, my dear, is my little secret! A lady needs her secrets, you know."

That would not do at all. She would make sure Granny spilled the gumballs. Vesuvia hated secrets—unless she was the one keeping them.

ICY MIST SPRAYED RICK'S FACE AS HE DANGLED OVER THE DARK RAVINE. AND THEN HE FELL, tumbling through the open air, letting out a pitiful wail. A circle of rope looped over his chest and pulled tight. The rope jerked him hard, but it stopped his fall.

Sprout stood at the edge of the cliff, holding the end of his lasso with impressive strength. He had snagged Rick just in time.

"I gotcha, partner," Sprout said with a cocky grin.

"Sprout, you saved me!" Rick cried, glad his glasses hid his tears. He wanted to look strong for his friend and hero.

Vesuvia and Evie appeared on either side of Sprout and hooked their arms around his shoulders, dressed in loud, outrageous outfits like the girls in *Animon Hunters*.

"Come on Sprout," Evie said. "It's not worth it. Let's go."

"Why, Evelyn, what a *fab*ulous idea!" Vesuvia walked away from the edge of the cliff. "I'll make us smoothies."

"Aww, shucks," Sprout said. "I could really go for one a them tasty drinks."

"No, Sprout! No!" Rick begged. "You don't need a smoothie!"

Sprout frowned. "Sorry, stranger. My friends need me." He let go of the lasso. Rick dropped.

"Not a smoothie!" he cried. "Evie, help! Noooo!"

Evie and Sprout stared into the pit as he fell. Rick tumbled through the air. But as he looked down, he didn't see water at all, but thick, sticky ink, like the stain in the Pacific. The stain his mother had gone to clean up.

As the wet blackness swallowed him, Rick awoke with a gasp. He pulled the blanket off from over his head. He rubbed his eyes as they adjusted to the light in the acorn escape pod. "Did I fall asleep?" he asked.

From the pilot's seat, 2-Tor nodded. "Your astute powers of observation continue to impress, young Richard. What were you dreaming about?"

Rick blushed. "You could tell I was dreaming?"

"I may no longer possess my sophisticated life-monitoring sensors, but I am no dodo, either. I heard you say your sister's name, and that boy's, Sprout. I also heard you articulate something about smoothies, but I assumed that was less important."

Rick felt around for his glasses. "I don't know, 2-Tor. I guess . . . Sprout was *my* friend, you know? Evie stole him away from me. And she's always putting down my ideas. She never seems to care that I put a lot of thought into making decisions . . . unlike her."

"Richard! It is time for a quiz."

"Ugh, not now, 2-Tor." Rick picked up the blanket and pillow but didn't see his glasses anywhere. It was one of the cruel ironies of life that you needed your glasses to find your glasses.

2-Tor waggled a feather. "Ah, ah, ah. Yes now. Question one: Why do you think Evelyn is so impulsive?"

"I don't know, 2-Tor."

"Have you ever stopped to think maybe it is because you are so meticulous?"

"But that doesn't make any sense!"

"It most certainly does make sense. You and Evelyn are both remarkably bright, but you think things through in a way few humans can. You are also both highly competitive. But Evie cannot compete with you in a data-centric way. So she blazes her own trail, to borrow an idiom from your Texan friend."

"You're saying Evie acts crazy on purpose."

"No, no, no! I am saying you think in different ways, neither better than the other. You should give her more credit, Richard. She often wonders why you do not take *her* ideas seriously."

"Because her ideas are *dumb,* 2-Tor."

The big crow gave him a look that, even on his birdy face, clearly said, *Do you see my point?*

At last Rick found his glasses hanging from the collar of his shirt. He put them on and saw the world much clearer.

The pilot's console beeped. "Oh!" 2-Tor said. "We are coming up on the stain."

An expanse of dark water bruised the ocean surface. The inky stain undulated with the waves. It was huge—bigger than a Hawaiian island. A number of Cleanaspot boats floated along the edge of the stain, their hulls black with the ink. The boats sprayed the stain with Mom's special eco-friendly cleaning solution, but the concoction seemed to be having no visible effect.

On the far side of the stain floated a sea vessel Rick had never seen before—a football-stadium-sized vial of ink. "2-Tor, whose ship is that?"

"That is an Ink-A-Spot transport vessel."

"Ink-A-Spot? Hmm . . . that seems convenient."

"Yes, it makes me moult to think that they accused your mother and Cleanaspot of creating the stain as a way to make a hefty profit from the cleanup job. To think that your mother would intentionally damage the oceans and then frame Ink-A-Spot . . . why, it's just preposterous! But what's your point, Richard?"

"Well, what does Ink-A-Spot do when they're not accusing my mother of crimes she didn't commit?"

"They carry ink, oil, and other hazardous materials across the ocean."

"So, in other words, there's basically no doubt that they're the ones who made the stain in the first place, right?"

"You are wise as an owl and sharp as a talon, my dear boy!"

"In that case," said Rick, "let's go get those guys." Using the sensors in the escape pod, Rick detected the homing beacon in his mother's phone. Sure enough, the signal was coming from the Ink-A-Spot ship. 2-Tor piloted the escape pod over to the ship and landed in one of its hangars.

"This place is busy," Rick remarked as he climbed out of the cramped escape pod. Everywhere he looked mechanics and robots scurried about the hangar deck, prepping hoverships for flight.

"They must be trying to hide their guilt by cleaning up the stain themselves," 2-Tor said. "After all, contaminating the oceans really could damage one's reputation."

A woman with a brown ponytail hurried over to Rick and 2-Tor. She wore spotless overalls with an insignia that read "Crew Chief." "Hey! You can't park that here. This is a restricted area." She pointed at 2-Tor. "And take that mask off. What do you think this is, Halloween?"

It was so hard for most people to believe that 2-Tor was actually a giant talking crow that they generally assumed what to them was the most logical explanation.

Rick patted 2-Tor on the wing. "My friend here was in a costume contest. There was a bit of a glitch. We accidentally sewed him into the bird suit."

"Bird suit!" 2-Tor squawked, offended. "I say."

"Wow!" the crew chief said. "Those animatronics are pretty cool."

"Thank you," Rick said. "Um . . . my father designed them? Speaking of my family, I'm trying to find my mother. Melinda Lane. Have you seen her?"

"The Cleanaspot woman? Oh kid, you better follow me."

She called to a group of mechanics on break. "Davis! Take over. I'll be right back. Let's go, kid."

The crew chief led Rick through the corridors of the Ink-A-Spot ship. Everything was immaculate. Not a single speck of dirt or smudge of grime was anywhere to be seen. Strange. He had expected it to be, well, inkier. The place reminded him of the Cleanaspot offices, and the visits he used to take there with his mother after preschool. Those trips were some of his fondest memories with his mother. She had always been there for him. He needed her now more than ever.

They reached an entrance to a restricted area, which at first Rick thought had no door—a rather strange way to enter a restricted area. But in fact there was a glass partition. It was just polished so clearly it was practically invisible. The glass slid aside as they entered.

Two glass desks acted as sentries on either side of this entry room. Behind the desks the secretaries wore long white robes and powdered wigs. A quartet of Winterpole agents in dark suits formed a line at the other end of the entry room.

Rick wanted to run, but where could he go? Winterpole must have known it was him and Evie who broke Vesuvia out of the Prison at the Pole. If they identified him, he'd be going back there real soon.

The crew chief waved goodbye and walked back to her hangar, while the Winterpole agents moved in closer.

"You're the son of Melinda Lane?" one of them asked. "The stainer?"

"The liar?"

"What's your name, boy?"

"Uh . . . um . . ." Rick tried to think of something to get him out of this mess.

"I say!" 2-Tor bellowed. "I do rightly say. Step back, agents. I know the law! I know Winterpole tribunal statutes like the back of my drumstick. I demand you let this boy see his mother at once, criminal or not! Who is in charge here?"

"Quit squawking, you costumed freak," said one of the agents, an older bald man with a hooked nose. "I'm Mister Horn. I'm in charge here."

"Costumed!?" 2-Tor said like someone had called him fat.

Mister Horn tried to lower the rising tempers. "All right, everyone calm down. The guy in the bird suit is right. The statutes clearly state that family can visit the prisoner the day before the trial."

"Trial?!" Rick cried.

"Bird suit?!" 2-Tor said, equally in horror.

"Well, come on," Mister Horn said, waving them to the back room. "This way."

Relieved, Rick felt the blood rush back to his head. The good news was that this division of Winterpole had not been notified of the break-in at the Prison at the Pole. As long as the agents stayed in the dark, Rick could stay out of trouble.

From what Rick could tell, Winterpole had been given space to operate on the Ink-A-Spot vessel. The architecture and furniture were all too clean and modern for Winterpole, but the people, with their stiff outfits and overly serious attitudes, were more what Rick expected.

They reached a heavy locked door with an entry keypad. Mister Horn shielded the keypad with his hand as he punched in a few numbers. The door opened and suddenly Rick was back at the Prison at the Pole.

Well, not quite. But it was a jail and did bring back those rotten memories.

Here the walls were made of glass and metal instead of ice, and cramped cells lined both sides of a narrow corridor. The cells were empty except for the one at the end, where Rick's mother was sitting on a thin cot, her head in her hands.

"Mom?"

She raised her head, a look of pure disbelief in her eyes. She ran to the bars of her cell and reached for her son. "Rick! Rick, my darling!"

"No touching!" snapped Mister Horn.

"Mom, are you all right? I have to get you out of here. We have to get back to the eighth continent. Everything is in danger. What happened to you?"

His mother sighed. "Oh, Rick, it was terrible. Cleanaspot has stripped me of my command."

"What? How can that be?"

She looked at 2-Tor expectantly and a silent understanding passed between them. "Yes, Mum," he said, nodding. Then he walked over to Mister Horn. "I say, I have a very complicated question about Statute Forty-Zero-A. Might you be able to clear things up for me?"

Mom lowered her voice and leaned close to Rick. "Ink-A-Spot accused us of creating the stain ourselves. They got Winterpole involved. Then Cleanaspot realized all of Winterpole was after was me. Probably revenge for something to do with your father and the eighth continent. Anyway, Cleanaspot had to distance itself from me so Winterpole would back off, but now people are saying that *I* created the stain by myself. How could that even be possible?" She sighed. "The Cleanaspot board says if I don't clean the stain by sundown, I'll lose my job forever."

"But it's *your* company," Rick said. "They can't fire you, can they?"

"They can. But that's not even the worst of it. Winterpole is going to put me on trial for creating the stain. That's why I'm stuck here. They're going to keep holding me captive until I am found guilty or innocent—but probably guilty. I don't know how to prove I didn't do it."

"Who is defending you at your trial? You need an advocate."

"I was going to do it myself, but"—Mom shook her head sadly—"Winterpole issued a gag order on me for the trial. I won't be able to speak."

"Mom . . . I can do this. I can defend you!"

"But Rick, you're just a boy. I can't ask you to—"

"—You won't be able to stop me," he said. "I'll start studying right away."

She reached her hand through the bars to touch his face. "I need you now more than ever, Rick."

"Hey!" Mister Horn shoved 2-Tor out of the way. "I said no touching."

2-Tor scratched his beak. "Ah, yes, I see. *Fifty*-Zero-A. Very illuminating."

That was all the time they were allowed with the prisoner. Mister Horn showed them out of Winterpole's makeshift office-slash-jail. Rick's head was spinning. Mom imprisoned. Dad missing. Evie off on her own.

This was exactly what Evie was trying to prevent—the family was all broken up.

But no more. Rick would find a way to bring the family back together and save the eighth continent. And if that meant taking on the entire Winterpole Tribunal system by himself, then that's what he was going to do.

DIANA STEPPED INTO ROOM Z-99 AND CLOSED THE DOOR. GEORGE LANE SAT IN THE CHAIR BEFORE her, slumped over in exhausted defeat.

A fish slid out of the bucket above him and landed on his head with a squish. George didn't even react.

Diana had told the Polar Bear she needed to see the prisoner to conduct research for the report her mother had requested. But, of course, that wasn't exactly true. Circling behind George, Diana switched off the torture device. The hum of the machine faded and suddenly the only audible sound was George Lane's shallow breathing. He tried to look back at her, but he was too weak to move. When he spoke, his voice was a whisper, barely audible. "What are you doing?"

Diana struggled with the ropes tying him to the chair. Her fingers were cold and the knots were tight. At last Diana managed to undo the bonds. "I'm getting you out of here. Try not to speak," she said as the ropes dropped to the floor. Diana pulled George to his feet and led him to the door, attempting to hold her breath. It wasn't his fault that he reeked of fish, but that didn't mean he smelled any less like the seafood section of the local supermarket.

The halls of the Prison at the Pole were quiet and empty. George was too weak to walk on his own, so Diana put his arm over her shoulder for support and helped him limp down the corridor. George looked at her quizzically, as if asking whether she was sure that she wanted to do this.

Diana nodded. Yes, she was sure. More sure than she'd been in a long time. She kept mentally replaying the fight she'd had with everyone back in Vesuvia's cell. She couldn't believe that her mother actually sided with Benjamin Nagg over her. The whole thing felt so typically Winterpole, but she'd have hoped that her mother would have cared about her enough to see reason.

Diana led George to the roof access doors at the end of the hall, taking most of his weight on her shoulders. She opened the doors and went up the stairs.

A few small hoverships were parked on the rooftop landing pad. One of the armed sentries approached.

"Where are you taking this man?" he asked.

Diana flashed him her identification card. "Prisoner transfer from room Z-99. Warden's instructions."

The guard grimaced. "Yikes. I wouldn't want to cross the Polar Bear today. Move along."

"Okay, thanks."

She helped Mister Lane lie down in the back of the hovership and then ignited the engines. It didn't matter what her mother thought anymore. Diana was through following orders from Winterpole.

EVIE SAW THE PINK ROBOTS EVEN BEFORE SHE SAW THE EIGHTH CONTINENT.

"Look at them rascals yonder." Sprout pointed out the front view screen of the *Roost*. The birds and flying fish and other robo-animals were spewing multicolored liquids of questionable origin.

"It's not going to be easy to sneak around them." Evie shook her head in dismay. Her mind was still crowded with regrets about her fight with Rick, but she had to focus on the mission at hand. She angled the *Roost* down. They plummeted through the clouds. Swirling white vapor rushed past the windshield. Then they broke into the clear. Directly below them, the *Big Whale* loomed. It was even bigger up close.

Evie screamed and pulled up hard on the *Roost*'s flight stick, missing the *Big Whale* so narrowly her hovership's leaves brushed the side of the blimp. "We got pink thingies on our tail!" *On our tail* was something Evie had always wanted to say in a hovership battle. In this case, however, the phrase was an understatement. The persistent robo-birds flung their payloads at the *Roost*, battering the aft of the hovership with noxious substances like acid, raw sewage, and high-fructose corn syrup. "Sprout, where do we need to plant the super root?"

"We've got to attach it to the underside of the continent all snug-like. That'll let it grow up and grow down at the same time."

"Sounds good!"

Evie directed the *Roost* toward the ocean surface. They had to root the continent right away. Even without Rick's countdown application, Evie knew they were out of time. She could see the eighth continent approaching Australia through the hovership window.

Sprout raised a nervous eyebrow. "Evie, what are you doing? You're heading right for the water. We're gonna be smashed flatter than a tomato under a boot!"

"You said we had to get under the continent. Well here we go!" The *Roost* picked up speed. Evie gripped the flight stick with all her strength. At the last second she pulled up, and the hovership skimmed along the surface of the water, coming to a stop close to the sandy shore of the eighth continent.

Evie engaged the autopilot and set it on a two-minute timer. She hurried to the storage hold, grabbed the super root that they'd stashed in a waterproof bag, and waved for Sprout to follow.

Together they opened the diving locker. They zipped on wetsuits, shouldered oxygen tanks, gathered heavy diving weights, and put on their scuba helmets. Evie stuck her pocket tablet in a waterproof case and strapped it to her wrist, so she could issue commands to the *Roost* underwater. Next she opened the thick bark gate and she and Sprout hopped in the water, clutching the weights to their chests.

As soon as they were deep enough, the *Roost* rocketed into the air and led the attacking robo-birds away.

Sprout's voice came in through the short-range communicator. "Yee-haw! It worked! Them robo-birds ain't following us no more."

Evie's sudden rush of relief morphed into a calm focus as the weights pulled them down through the dark, cold water. For the first time, she saw the underside of the eighth continent. From down here, it looked almost like an egg in a nest, the last remaining vestiges of garbage cupping the natural earth and sand. The Eden Compound must not have reached the trash under here—it was still the Great Pacific Garbage Patch.

Winterpole, the return of Vesuvia, and now this—Evie was starting to realize that bad things never went away for good. It was not a comforting notion.

Once they had descended enough to swim under the continent, Evie and Sprout released the diving weights. They tumbled into the depths, but just as they were about to fade from view, a big pink blur swam beneath them and swallowed the weights in one quick bite.

Evie and Sprout shared a frightened look. *Chompedo!*

They kicked frantically through the water. Maybe, just maybe, if they hurried to the underside of the continent, they could not only root it but also find a place to hide where Chompedo wouldn't be able to get to them. Reaching out a hand, Evie grabbed at the mangled bicycles and broken inventions closest to her. She wormed her way through the twisted metal and plastic, pulling herself inside the hard bramble. Sprout followed her and Chompedo tried to do the same.

Evie held her breath as the robo-shark slammed into the trash—once, twice, three times to no avail. *He can't break through!* Evie realized. Their unspoken plan had worked.

Chompedo floated in the water, staring up at Evie and Sprout hungrily. From this perspective, Evie could see that the giant shark was damaged. One of his eyes was completely smashed, and his pink hull was dented in a dozen places, the paint scraped and abraded, presumably as a result of the impromptu EMP she and Rick had built during the Piffle Pink Patrol's assault.

Chompedo slammed into the tangled garbage, denting it and breaking off pieces. He stuck his nose through this new hole like a dog, trying to wriggle his way to Evie. When that didn't work, he bared his chainsaw teeth and tried to cut through the metal, but some of his teeth were broken and others were missing.

Hmm . . . probably not worth it to test the robot's capabilities, Evie thought. "Sprout, let's hurry!" she said.

The trashy base of the continent was too dense to swim through; they had to squeeze through the metal root system like it was an oversized jungle gym. Soon they reached the top, where the metal and plastic turned into the spongy earth of the post-Eden Compound continent.

"Plant the bulb here," Sprout said through the radio in his scuba helmet. He unzipped the top of his wetsuit, took the bulb out of his pocket, and handed it to her. "I reckon it'll start to grow as soon as we introduce it to the soil."

This was the moment Evie had been waiting for. She only wished her family were there to see it. She scooped out a handful of earth and smooshed the root into the hole, then packed the earth back in place. The plastic and scrap metal beneath them thrummed as Chompedo repeatedly rammed into it.

Evie watched in anticipation as the first tendrils of vine curled out of the dirt. The vines spiraled through the metal and plastic, spreading. One of the longer roots struck Chompedo as it reached down. Lucky for them, Chompedo took that as his signal to flee from the pugnacious root.

The vines grew thicker, pushing Evie and Sprout apart. The kids climbed away from the growing tendrils of root. Checking her pocket tablet, Evie brought up the *Roost*'s external camera. The vines had broken through the surface of the continent, and plants were popping up all over.

We did it! Evie thought. It reminded Evie of that fateful moment when they'd showered the Eden Compound down on the garbage patch and transformed it into her beloved continent. Only last time, Rick had been at her side and her parents had swooped in at the last moment. It didn't feel the same without them.

She hailed the *Roost* to come pick up her and Sprout. Soon they were back aboard and toweling their wet hair dry.

The effect of the super root was even more impressive when seen in person. Evie watched the vines tear through the Winterpole camp, smashing buildings to bits.

But something wasn't right. The continent was still drifting closer toward the Australian coast.

"Why hasn't it stopped moving?" Evie asked in dismay.

Sprout wrinkled his forehead. "We wanted to use the root as an anchor, right?"

"Yeah . . ."

"Well, there must not be anything for the root to connect to on the ocean floor. We need to attach it to something."

"But what?" Evie thought about it but got nowhere. This was exactly the kind of thing Rick was good at, coming up with plans that worked even when she felt like they shouldn't. His brain was so stuffed full of facts, and his little computer programs were always so helpful. She regretted now, more than ever, how much she'd argued with him and hadn't appreciated his ideas.

Suddenly, Evie had an idea of her own. "Sprout," she said. "I've got it. I know how to anchor the continent for good."

WITHOUT A PICOSECOND TO SPARE, RICK PUSHED OPEN THE HEAVY DOORS INTO THE COURTROOM where the tribunal was being held.

No one seemed to notice.

The room was curved like an old Greek amphitheater, with steps leading down to a flat stage at the bottom. Behind this stage was a large structure where three tribunes in powdered wigs witnessed arguments.

The Winterpole Advocate, whose only job was to convince the tribunes that Rick's mom was a bad person, had just completed his closing statement.

"I believe we have heard testimony to our satisfaction," said the first tribune. He glanced dismissively at Rick's mother, who sat on the floor, her arms bound by a squid-cuff. "Shall we render a verdict?"

"I submit an affirmative," stated the second tribune.

"Then let us proceed," the third tribune agreed.

Rick shouted from the top of the chamber. "You will not proceed! I object!"

The first tribune rose from his padded leather armchair and slammed his gavel against his desk. "No one may object without the proper permission slip. Silence!"

Where the gavel struck, a shockwave emanated. These devices detected sound waves and reflected the reverse waveform of whatever sound they picked up—the latest in noise-canceling technology.

But Rick was holding a large piece of cyber paper, curled at the bottom like a long scroll. The cyber paper thrummed like a gong, deflecting the noise-canceling attack.

"You will *not* silence me!" Rick bellowed. "I have permission to speak!"

He and 2-Tor had spent the whole day speed reading Winterpole legal books and submitting applications for permission slips. Now he was ready to make the case to free his mom and then get back to the eighth continent. Rick was packing paper.

"Come down here, boy," said the Winterpole Advocate. "There's no need to resist justice. These good tribunes know Mrs. Lane is guilty. You must accept reality."

"I demand proof of evidence!" Rick raced down the steps to the tribunal stage, past several stern-faced executives from Ink-A-Spot in the audience. He flung his completed request forms at the wigged tribunes. The cyber paper sheets landed in front of them and switched on, illuminating holographic projections of his list of demands. "I've done the research into this matter. Has the tribunal? There is no evidence linking Mrs. Lane to the stain. In fact, she has a solid alibi—she was nowhere near the stain's origin point when it formed."

"Objection!" The Winterpole Advocate stomped his foot. "Just because she wasn't near the stain doesn't mean she wasn't behind its creation."

Rick pulled an index card from his breast pocket and flung it at the advocate. "Permission to speak freely!" he shouted.

The cyber paper card fluttered toward the advocate and slapped against his face, sealing his mouth shut. It had taken Rick hours of filling out a fifty-page form to acquire a Winterpole gag order, but it was worth it. It would buy him the time he needed to make his case.

Rick cleared his throat. "Ahem. Furthermore, the stain is composed of Ink-A-Spot's trademark stain solution UberDark-X. The chemical makeup of this solution is a closely guarded corporate secret. Mrs. Lane never had, nor will she ever have, knowledge of this formula, nor the means to fabricate it herself."

The Winterpole Advocate shoved Rick out of the way. "Mmph hmph mrff! Muffph!" he said. The gag order still blocked his sneering lips.

The first tribune leaned forward. "I believe what the advocate is trying to say is that Mrs. Lane may have fabricated the stain to frame Ink-A-Spot. We have testimony from a Cleanaspot employee claiming as much."

"Who at Cleanaspot made these accusations?"

"Well, ergh . . ." the tribunes stammered and shuffled their papers.

"If you cannot produce the witness, then there is nothing connecting Mrs. Lane to the stain. She and the ocean are the victims here. Not Ink-A-Spot. In fact, without the witness, we can safely assume that this Cleanaspot accuser doesn't exist."

"They do exist!" the Winterpole Advocate insisted, having finally removed his gag. "They were provided to us by Ink-A-Spot."

"Ink-A-Spot?" the second tribune repeated.

Rick banged his hand down against the bench, like a gavel of his own. "Well, that just goes to show who the real culprit is."

The third tribune beckoned for the Winterpole Advocate to approach the bench. "The boy is right. Produce the witness, or this tribunal is over."

The advocate massaged his red lips. "My employer says I don't have to produce anything."

"Your employer? You mean Winterpole itself?!" The three tribunes looked equally outraged. "Case dismissed!"

"On what grounds?!" The Ink-A-Spot executives in the audience rose from their seats, looking quite outraged.

"Lack of evidence!" the tribunes said, slamming their gavels in unison.

The security agents disabled the squid-cuff binding Rick's mother's hands. She raced to Rick and took him into her arms, showering him with mushy kisses. "You did it, my baby. You did it, you did it!"

"M-o-m! Stop!" Rick tried to cover his cheeks.

"I will not stop! Smooch!"

Rick was in a daze. The tribunal had taken a lot out of him. But he'd done it. He'd beaten Winterpole at their own game.

After a brief trip on the acorn escape pod, Rick, his mom, and 2-Tor landed on the flagship of the Cleanaspot fleet, the *Sudsy Bubbler*. Catherine was waiting for them, cradling her computer tablet. She gave Rick a high five as he hopped out of the acorn escape pod and onto the deck. "I'm so glad you're all right, ma'am," she said, handing the tablet to Rick's mom, who examined the device quickly as they walked inside the ship. "I can't believe the Cleanaspot board was going to fire you over this stain. They must be getting nasty pressure from Winterpole to pull a stunt like that. But don't worry. Everyone on the *Sudsy Bubbler* is loyal to you, ma'am."

They reached the conference room, just aft of the bridge. Long windows on either side of the bright room let in the sea breeze—the salty smell reminding Rick of mornings on the shores of the eighth continent. He longed to return to his new home soon.

No one blinked when a seven-foot-tall talking crow entered the room. Cleanaspot executives were used to the eccentricities of the Lane family.

Mom took her seat at the head of the large conference table. To Rick's surprise, she offered him the seat at her side. "This is the only place my hero should be," she said, smiling. Rick wondered if this was how the heroes in his video games felt after beating the last level. But deep down he knew their troubles weren't over yet.

2-Tor perched on a chair and started pecking at the mountain of doughnuts laid out on the table. Crumbs and blobs of sugary icing spilled across the smooth tabletop. The Cleanaspot executives watched the crow in horror—birdliness they could excuse; messiness they could not.

Catherine began a slideshow to catch them up on the latest with the stain. "The black blob has not been responding to any of the usual treatments. It's quite vexing, Mrs. Lane. It's almost like the stain doesn't want to be cleaned up, like it's fighting us."

"Double the amount of eco-cleaner in the water boats. Surely the stain will react to one of our products."

"We've already tripled the amount of eco-cleaner, Mrs. Lane."

Mom wrinkled her brow. "Hmm . . . can we reroute boats from other cleanup jobs? The stain has to be the biggest job we have going on right now. Let's get all hands on deck."

Catherine shook her head. "We could try that, but some of those boats are days away. We don't have that kind of time."

Rick's mom turned to him. "Got any ideas, honey?"

He thought carefully for a moment, applying all the analysis and calculations he could muster. There had to be some way to get rid of the stain. But what?

Suddenly, Rick remembered a fascinating book he had

read recently on solvents. "What if we add water to the stain? Try to dilute it into a more manageable solution."

Mom's forehead wrinkled. "You want us to add water to the stain? But it's in the ocean."

"Yeah," Catherine said. "That's about as diluted as it gets. But it's still not breaking up the stain."

Rick polished his glasses, thinking. "Hm, good point. Well, I could do some research and try to find a new formula to break up inky compounds."

Mom smiled. "Great. Can you do it by sundown?"

"Um, well, honestly . . . probably not."

Rick was beginning to realize that he was going about this all wrong. He was trying to use logic and reason to solve the problem, but what he needed was creative, outside-the-box thinking. Whenever Rick tried to think that way, as soon as he came up with one bad idea, he stopped, because it seemed illogical to pursue bad ideas.

Across the conference table, 2-Tor was watching him, an expectant look on his avian face. The crow was trying to tell him something.

"We should ask Evie if she has any suggestions," Rick blurted out suddenly.

Mom raised an eyebrow. "Evie? Why?"

"She's always coming up with crazy ideas. And thinking about this problem logically isn't working. Maybe what we need a crazy idea. Maybe what we need is Evie."

"SO YOU SEE, WE'RE ALL STUMPED HERE, AND WE WANTED TO KNOW—I WANTED TO KNOW—IF YOU had any ideas."

Evie listened carefully, watching her brother's face on her pocket tablet. She stood outside the *Roost*, looking across the landscape of the eighth continent. A rocky cliff was just ahead, overhanging a deep ravine. As soon as she and Sprout had gotten back to the *Roost*, they'd flown to a remote corner of the continent in an attempt to hide their tree-shaped ship among its jagged cliffs while they tried to come up with a way to anchor the super root to the ocean floor. To make matters worse, Winterpole had launched a counter-attack against the *Big Whale*. The lights of pink robots battling hoverships filled the sky. Evie's mind felt like the sky must have felt—mayhem full of flashing lights and clashing ideas.

"Listen, Rick, about before, I—"

"Evie, I know, but we don't have much time."

"Okay." The wind was whipping her ponytail—blowing stray wisps of hair across her face. She had to think. How could she anchor the continent, sop up the stain, help Mom, and save the day? Even with so much at stake, Evie's mind wandered. It was hard to believe Rick and their mom had come to *her* for help.

Gazing across the open expanses of her continent, Evie wondered what this area had been before the Eden Compound changed it. Sometimes she would look at a cylindrical rock formation and immediately see a tower of old car tires. But sometimes it was just wide stretches of the spongy green earth.

Spongy earth. The ground did have a lot of give to it, but it sprung back into place when she raised her foot. The dirt on the eighth continent had a number of strange properties. This was only one of them. Evie could shovel the dirt, kick it, or pack it like normal dirt. But it was different too. She remembered the way the continent drank up all the weird ingredients the Piffle Pink Patrol threw at it, from water and juice to olive oil and tapioca. The continent absorbed everything. Like a sponge.

Evie shouted into her tablet with a look of pure joy on her face. "That's it! Like a sponge, Rick! A sponge!"

Sprout stuck his head out of the *Roost*, raising an eyebrow. "What's all the hollering about?"

On the screen, Rick scratched his head. "Yeah, Evie, I have no idea what you're saying."

"No time to explain! But I've got it. Trust me."

"Evie, wait! You have to—" Rick disappeared as Evie pressed the button to end the call.

She turned to Sprout, who was sauntering toward her. "We need to soak up the stain somehow. And the eighth continent is spongy like a sponge."

"As opposed to spongy like a brick?" Sprout grinned.

Evie snorted in amusement. "We can use the continent to sop up the stain. We just need to get the continent over there."

"Well, saddle up, little lady," Sprout said. "I'm gonna hogtie this here continent and drag her home!"

They flew the *Roost* away from the battle raging between Condo Corp and Winterpole, landing again just offshore. A quick scuba dive later, they had taken the longest root dangling off the bottom of the continent and fastened it to the back of the *Roost*. Evie turned up the throttle until the hovership growled in exertion. She fired the engines.

The *Roost* took to the air, tugging the root tight. The tiny hovership pulled and pulled. Fortunately for Evie, Winterpole and Condo Corp were so caught up in their battle over the eighth continent, they didn't notice they weren't over the continent any more. The *Roost* was making off with the prize!

As the *Roost* pulled the continent, Evie scratched her chin the way Dad always did. Dad. He was still nowhere to be found. Rick had rescued Mom, no thanks to Evie, but Dad had disappeared and they hadn't even had a second to look for him. In his absence, a twist had appeared in Evie's heart. She felt responsible.

All Evie could do was focus on her mission for now, or

she would start to feel the twist getting tighter.

The going was slow at first, but soon the *Roost* picked up speed and the continent was cruising along the water like an inner tube behind a speedboat. They were halfway across the ocean when the hovership's sensors picked up the Winterpole patrol behind them. A flock of their hoverships was in hot pursuit, led by a bulky flying vehicle.

"Oh, sixteen kinds of darn it!" Evie moaned. "Now we're sunk for sure."

They promptly received a transmission from the lead hovership. A stiff, professional voice came over the comm. "You with the continent! On behalf of Winterpole we order you to proceed at a pace infinitely slower than the pace at which you are proceeding now. In other words, not at all!"

Evie grabbed the communicator. "But you don't understand! There's an enormous stain in the Pacific that's hurting the ocean. We're trying to clean it up. And the continent was on a collision course with Australia. We just wanted to pull it away. Don't you see? We're trying to protect the oceans, and Australia, and we're trying to make the continent stop moving so Winterpole can stop hounding the Lane family!"

She listened carefully as some quiet murmurs came over the comm. Clearly the agents aboard the lead hovership were discussing something.

"I know, Barry. She makes a couple of good points."

"Sure, Larry. I agree. But that doesn't mean we should let her run off with the continent."

"That's cold, Barry. Real cold."

"Oh you are at it again!"

Evie and Sprout exchanged a puzzled look.

"Well, we've checked the statutes," Agent Larry said. "Turns out there's nothing in the Winterpole bylaws prohibiting you from stealing a continent. I guess no one ever thought that would come up."

"Make a note of it!" Barry said.

"It's *our* continent!" Evie said.

Larry coughed. "Right. So. Can't stop you from taking the continent, and your story about cleaning up the oceans, that's cool with us."

"LARRY!" Barry shouted, annoyed.

"Sorry. We are okay with you pursuing this eco-friendly mission. Sheesh, Barry. Chill—"

"—Don't you say it!"

Evie leaned into the throttle. The engine argued, but she kept it up. "Okay, well thank you! Nice speaking to you gentlemen! So long, now."

The Winterpole agents continued to bicker as Evie and Sprout pulled the eighth continent closer to the stain—and to their final victory.

WITH A HEAVY THUD, THE *ROOST* LANDED ON THE DECK OF THE *SUDSY BUBBLER*. A FINAL, PITIFUL gasp emerged from the hover engine. Black smoke billowed from every opening on the vessel. But the thick root trailing from the hovership remained intact. The continent floated in the ocean, just beyond the edge of the stain.

Rick watched Sprout and Evie exit the *Roost*, looking pretty thrilled their long journey had finally come to an end. And in the nick of time, too. The sun was beginning to set, striping the western horizon in pink haze. They didn't have long before Cleanaspot would revoke Mom's command.

This urgency did not seem to be on Mom's mind as she sprinted across the deck to her daughter. She scooped Evie up in her arms, showering her with kisses all over her face. "Oh my darling! I'm so glad you're safe!"

"M-o-m! Stop!" Evie tried to cover her cheeks.

"I will not stop! Smooch!"

"There's no time! We have to soak up the stain before sundown!"

"Evie's right, Mom," Rick said, coming up behind, along with the others. "We have to hurry."

"Quite so!" 2-Tor added.

Mom put Evie down. "Okay. I know. Catherine! Connect this continent to the *Sudsy Bubbler* and let's move!"

The Cleanaspot workers scurried across the deck, detaching the continent from the *Roost* and re-attaching it to their flagship, which was a much more stable tugboat.

With the adults distracted, Rick stepped closer to Evie. "Hey."

Evie grinned. "'Evie's right.' I like the sound of that."

"Yeah, well, this whole thing was your idea. Including, it seems, completely destroying the *Roost*."

"Destroying?" She waved her hand at the *Roost*. "Psshh. She might look like she's in rough shape, but it's nothing an engine replacement and complete interior redesign won't fix."

"Interior redesign?"

"Yeah, but that's just because of the fires."

"Wait, *fires*, as in, plural?"

Evie rolled her eyes. "Rick! It was just a couple of them." Sprout nudged Evie, urging her to continue. With a sigh, Evie looked down at her feet. "Yeah, so, Rick, about before, I'm sorry we fought."

"Yeah, I'm sorry I'm always blaming you for everything," Rick said. "And to you too, Sprout. I just wanted you to be *my* best friend. I wish I hadn't acted like that."

2-Tor flapped his wings. "I say, that is wonderful news.

Everything is all patched up."

"It's my fault too," Evie said, turning to Sprout. "For the same reason. I wanted you to be my best friend."

Sprout tipped back his hat. "Aw, shucks, y'all. I reckon that's the silliest thing I ever heard. I'm both y'all's friend. Wouldn't have it any other way. Shoot, a week ago I was just a humble cabbage rancher with nothing going on. Now look at all the fun we've had!"

Rick smiled. If Sprout's idea of fun was outrunning robots, busting juvenile delinquents out of jail, and nearly dying in multiple fires, then he was going to fit right in with the Lane family.

Sprout looked between them. "As for best friends, why, that's sillier than a skydiving squash! Y'all both already have a best friend, and it sure ain't me."

Rick wrinkled his brow. "Who?"

"He means me, you nerd." Evie glowered.

Sprout was right of course. It was what 2-Tor had been trying to say. Rick and Evie were very different, but they complemented each other. They were stronger together than they were apart. They never could have accomplished their missions alone.

Suddenly 2-Tor scooped both kids up in his wings. "Oh I am so glad everyone is back safe and sound. My feathers could not take any more anxiety!"

Mom ran over to them. "All right, kids. Ready to see the world's biggest sponge in action?" She tapped her communicator. "Catherine! Increase speed to full throttle!"

The *Sudsy Bubbler* lurched, churning water with its big propellers. The root went tight.

Rick and Evie high-fived. Sprout gave them both a big hug.

But something was wrong. The continent wasn't moving.

They looked. It was hard to see at first, because it sort of blended in with the pink haze on the horizon.

"By my endless consternation!" 2-Tor moaned.

Rick couldn't have said it better himself. There in the distance was the *Big Whale*, tethered to a different tendril of the super root. Vesuvia's giant blimp was pulling the eighth continent in the other direction!

EVIE WATCHED IN DISMAY AS THE *SUDSY BUBBLER* AND THE *BIG WHALE* PLAYED TUG-OF-WAR WITH her continent.

"We have to fight them!" she said.

Rick grabbed her. "We have to run."

"What, why?"

"RUN!"

A tornado of pink robo-birds came screeching out of the sky. Evie and the others fled for cover. The Cleanaspot sailors turned their water cannons on the birds, but without more powerful defenses, fighting them was like trying to shoot a swarm of mosquitoes with a squirt gun.

They ran along the edge of the deck, teetering over the water far below. The birds flew all around them, pecking with their needle-sharp beaks. Evie shielded her face from the birds and shouted orders. "Mom! Have your people hold off the robots as long as they can. Rick! Sprout! Get to one of the acorns and take off. We have to stop Vesuvia!"

2-Tor squawked. "I say, Miss Evelyn. What shall I do?"

Evie screamed, "2-Tor, you gotta fly!"

"My word. What do you mean?"

"Fly, you bird. Fly!" Evie tackled 2-Tor, hurling both of them off the end of the boat.

2-Tor flapped his wings as they fell, slowing their descent and eventually gaining height. Evie clung to the bird's back. They left the *Sudsy Bubbler* far behind and far below.

"Get closer!" Evie yelled over the roaring wind, pointing ahead at the looming *Big Whale*.

The blimp's engines were going full reverse, pulling the vine like a dog with a chew toy. Evie squinted. Through the wide front viewport, she could see the determined faces of Vesuvia and Grandma Condolini.

"Come on, 2-Tor! Full flap ahead!" The flock of birds was right behind them and gaining.

They neared the viewport. "Miss Evelyn, I beg of you, please reconsider this line of attack. I swear, I would sooner be prohibited from administering quizzes for the rest of my days than proceed with this action."

"Relax, 2-Tor, we'll be fine!"

"Somehow I doubt that."

Behind the viewport, Vesuvia was glaring at Evie and gritting her artificially whitened teeth, but as 2-Tor flapped harder and picked up speed, that determined look morphed into one of incredulous shock. Evie had seen the Piffle Pink Patrol do this to the *Roost* once. She felt it was only appropriate to return the favor.

2-Tor and Evie crashed through the viewport. Glass shattered and whipped around the windy bridge, while the pursuing robo-birds flew in after them. The birds pierced the floor, the walls, and the command console. Grandma Condolini howled angrily as one of the birds hit the throttle, locking it at maximum. The engines roared and the blimp groaned.

Evie let go of 2-Tor and dropped into a somersault. She bounced to her feet and turned to face her enemy.

Vesuvia struggled to her feet. Her clothes were a mess. She plucked a little bird from her hair and threw it at the ground with a plastic *thok!* "You . . ." she hissed. "You ruin everything! GET HER!"

The serving-bots dropped their trays and moved in to attack. 2-Tor flapped his wings. "Shoo! Shoo!"

Evie made a break for the command console and grabbed the steering wheel. Grandma Condolini swatted at her. "Stop that, you little rodent! Let go!"

Evie pulled back as hard as she could. The *Big Whale* veered upward, tipping the bridge back at a steep angle. The serving-bots slid across the floor and slammed into the back wall. Grandma Condolini fell out of her chair. "Aie! My osteoporosis!"

Vesuvia grabbed Evie and pried her away from the controls. "Give me back my blimp!"

"Give me back my continent!" Evie said, fighting against the wind as she climbed on top of the command console and hopped out of the shattered viewport. The water was hundreds of feet below. One wrong step and it would be bye-bye Evie, hello pancakes.

Vesuvia climbed out the viewport after her, clinging to the nose of the *Big Whale*. "Hold still, Evie. It's time for you to go on a trip."

"I say, leave her alone!" came 2-Tor's voice. He'd followed Vesuvia out of the viewport, flapping his wings at her.

At that moment, the acorn escape pod flew by. Rick was piloting. Sprout leaned out the window. "Evie! What should we do?"

"You should catch her!" Vesuvia yelled, breaking free of 2-Tor and shoving Evie with all her might. Evie grabbed Vesuvia's arms, but the damage was done. They fell off the front of the *Big Whale* together.

Evie landed on the super root and scrambled to get a grip as she nearly slid off the taut tether. She winced, but managed to hold on. Vesuvia hit the root flat on her back.

"I have had it up to here with you." Vesuvia struggled to her feet, smoothing her loose bleached hair against her head. "You have ruined my *life*, Evie Lane. I *hate* you! And your stupid clothes! And your stupid shoes! And your stupid family! And that stupid bird! I hate you! And now I'm going to send you all to the bottom of the ocean where you belong."

"Evie, catch!" The acorn flew by again, and Sprout flung his machete at the root. It landed point down, embedded halfway up the blade.

As Evie drew the machete out of the root, Vesuvia watched in horror. "No! Don't do that. Stop!"

With a hard swipe, Evie cut deep into the root. She hacked at it, making the split deeper and wider.

"Don't!" Vesuvia begged.

Evie struck the root again and again, with each cut shouting, "Vesuvia! I! Like! These! Shoes!"

The machete sang as it sliced through the root. The *Big Whale*, now untethered, rocketed into the stratosphere. If they were lucky, the *Big Whale* would fly all the way to the moon, taking Vesuvia and Grandma Condolini along with it.

2-Tor dove clear of the blimp just in time. He arrowed toward Evie and nabbed her out of the sky before she hit the water.

The acorn flew alongside them. "You did it!" Rick cheered.

Evie waved the machete at them. "We did it!"

As they flew back to the Cleanaspot fleet, the *Sudsy Bubbler* pulled the eighth continent over the stain. Just like Evie expected, the spongy continent slurped up the ink with ease. She nodded, content and a little impressed with herself. "That worked pretty well, actually." Now they just needed to root their continent to the coral reef under the stain, and their new home would have a permanent address.

They landed back on the deck of the *Sudsy Bubbler*. Cleanaspot sailors were sweeping up piles of the pink robo-birds and depositing them in recycling containers. As Rick and Evie climbed out of the acorn escape pod, Mom came running over to them.

"Oh no, not again!" Evie said.

Mom scooped them up and smooched them like crazy.

The wet reunion was interrupted by the arrival of a Winterpole hovership, which touched down next to the acorn.

Evie let out a heavy sigh. Now what?

The cockpit door opened and Dad stepped into the light.

Mom squealed and ran to her husband, kissing him all over the face.

Dad's eyes went wide with panic. "Wah! Kids! Grab the mop!"

There were no mops in sight, so instead Rick and Evie ran and hugged their father. Sprout and 2-Tor watched the reunion, smiling (although 2-Tor had a beak and couldn't really smile).

Rick adjusted his glasses as he pulled away from the hug. "How did you get here? I thought Winterpole had you."

"I was trapped at the Prison at the Pole," Dad explained. "But this young lady helped me escape." He pointed to the open cockpit door.

Diana Maple stepped out.

"Diana?" Rick sounded as confused as Evie felt. "But you're . . ."

"Yeah, I know," Diana said awkwardly. "But it didn't feel right to keep your dad locked up. He didn't do anything wrong! Winterpole has been acting so weird lately."

"Lately?" Evie asked. Rick nudged her to hush up.

Dad smiled as he pulled Mom close. "Diana doesn't want to work for Winterpole anymore. And she doesn't want to work for Condo Corp either."

Diana nodded. "They really drive me nuts."

"You can stay here with us," Rick said. "You can help us build our civilization on the eighth continent. And you know how Condo Corp and Winterpole operate. You'd be a valuable asset."

"Sheesh, Rick," Evie elbowed her brother, "she's a person, not a beach house."

Rick smiled. "Either way, you're always welcome on Octopia."

"Octopia?" Evie shoved him playfully. "Is that your new name for the eighth continent? I kind of like that."

Rick looked hopeful. "Really?"

"No, of course not. That name is stupid. You might as well call it Squid City."

Dad flailed his hands in the air. "No more squids, please! No sea creatures of *any kind*, thank you."

"Y'all could name the eighth continent *Ocho*," Sprout suggested, prompting thoughtful nods from Rick and Evie.

Diana smiled at them. "Whatever you decide to call it, I'm not sure I can leave Winterpole just yet. My mom is there, and . . . I dunno. I can be more help to you if I'm at Winterpole, on the inside. I'll stay to deflect suspicion, and I can keep you up to date on whatever crazy schemes they're up to."

"A double agent!" Evie cheered.

"Something like that."

"Well, good luck," Rick said.

"Yeah, good luck," Evie echoed. "Oh, and when you get back to Winterpole, can you please tell them that the Lanes are once again sovereign owners of the continent?"

Everyone smiled. It was a hard-fought victory. But their troubles, at least for now, were over.

"I'll tell them for sure!" Diana said as she climbed back aboard the hovership. "And I'll see you again soon. I promise."

When Diana had flown away, Sprout began to fidget anxiously.

"What's wrong, Sprout?" Evie asked as she and Rick stepped close to him.

"Well shoot, y'all. This has been one grand adventure—finer than fresh berries, if I say so. But I should really be packing it back to the Prof."

Evie couldn't believe it. "You . . . you're leaving?"

Sprout removed his hat solemnly. "Just for a while, I reckon. The Prof needs me for the growing season. But I want y'all to know that I ain't never had two finer friends in my whole life. No finer family, neither."

A stubborn tear fell from Evie's eye. She flung her arms around Sprout, and Rick joined in on the hug.

"I'll be seeing you soon, amigos." Sprout backed away and strolled west toward the bow of the ship. "On the other side of the sunset."

Evie and Rick watched sadly as he departed. Sprout took

about ten steps, then stopped, turned, and walked quickly back to his friends.

"Um . . ." he mumbled. "I just realized—can any of y'all give me a ride back to Texas?"

THOSE UGLY, STUPID LANES, VESUVIA THOUGHT, AS SHE FLOATED ALONE IN THE MIDDLE OF THE ocean. *This is all their fault.*

She clung to a floating lump of vine that had broken off when Evie cut the root. Vesuvia had hung on for dear, sweet, precious life, but when the *Big Whale*'s engines blew out, she rode that puppy straight into the sea.

How had she ended up here, *again*?

A short way off from her flotation plant, a pink dorsal fin emerged from the water. It moved toward her, cutting a narrow wake.

Chompedo splashed out of the water and reared up in front of her.

"Chompedo! Thank goodness. Get me out of this cold, wet whatever-it-is."

The hatch on top of Chompedo opened and Granny stuck her head out. "Ocean. It's called the ocean, Susu."

Vesuvia growled. "Shut up, Granny! I know what it's called."

A minute later, Vesuvia slumped into a chair at the front of the compartment inside Chompedo. The industrial-strength hair dryer she had installed blasted her dry and fluffy again. "UGGGGH. I wanna go *home*, Granny."

"Not yet," Granny said, inputting some new coordinates into Chompedo's computer. "We still have work to do."

"Work? UGGGGH."

Granny ignored Vesuvia's articulate protests and watched through the front portholes as Chompedo sank beneath the waves. They cruised through the deep waters of the ocean. Vesuvia was fuming. Granny Venoma was hissing. Those cursed Lanes. They ruined everything.

Then, out of the darkness, a black robo-shark appeared. Vesuvia couldn't see all of it in the murky depths, but it was so big it made Chompedo look like a guppy. It made the *Big Whale* look like a small whale. It was larger than any robot she had ever seen.

"Granny . . . Granny! We're heading right for that thing. Change course!"

The old woman faced Vesuvia and gave her a quiet look, then returned her gaze to the front portholes. The black shark's jaws unhinged. Chompedo swam into its gullet.

Vesuvia's pink shark surfaced at a steel dock in a cybernetically enhanced cavern. Blinking lights on the gnarled machines were the only illumination in the dim space. Robotic grabbing arms locked Chompedo in a berth, extended an exit ramp, and twisted the access hatch open.

Vesuvia and her grandmother emerged to find a very unpleasant-looking welcoming committee.

Twelve guards stood like toy soldiers in a row. They carried huge assault rifles in their arms and wore military uniforms as black as the stain on the Pacific had been. Stylish and deadly, just the way Vesuvia liked. It was clear these were not the bumbling agents of Winterpole. These were deadly, terrifying men.

Standing in front of the guards was a man in a suit. It was strange, but that was the only thing she could really identify about him. Sure, when she stared at him closely she could tell that he had ghost-pale skin and craggy cheeks, but as soon as she looked away, those features faded, like details from a dream, and she was left with a single image. The suit.

"Ah, Mister Dark, hello again. Ooh, my back." Granny stepped down the exit ramp and approached the man.

Vesuvia followed her. "You know this department-store mannequin?"

"Quiet, Susu!" Granny snapped.

Mister Dark gave Granny a look that matched his name. "You have disappointed us, Madame Condolini. You were supposed to extract the Eden Compound from the continent and bring it to us."

"Did you *see* what we had to put up with? Antagonists at every turn!" Granny showed her best annoyed-with-you face, but there was something about her tone and the look in her eyes that told Vesuvia something was wrong. She was frightened.

Mister Dark saw it too. "We created the stain on the Pacific as a diversion, and still you failed. A handful of children and Winterpole proved to be too much for you. How disappointing."

Granny's panic grew. "Mister Dark, please. You don't understand. There was this bird, and—"

Pulling out his pocket tablet, Mister Dark tapped on it, examining a digital control panel.

"Hey!" Granny said. "Look at me when I'm talking to you. Don't play with your phone."

Mister Dark didn't look up. "I'm not playing." He tapped a button on the screen.

A hole opened in floor under Granny's feet and she fell. "Susu!!!" she screamed, but Vesuvia didn't even have time to reach for her. Granny was gone faster than a limited release of designer shoes. The hole in the floor closed again.

The footsteps of Mister Dark echoed loudly as he approached Vesuvia. She held her ground. "We've been watching you, Vesuvia Piffle. For a long time."

"Shocker," she said with a snort. "No one can take their eyes off of me."

He leaned over her. She flinched. "Aw. Are you afraid of me, little lady?"

Vesuvia glared. "I'm afraid of what I might do to you if you don't back off."

Mister Dark stared at her, unsmiling. "I'm not here to hurt you, Vesuvia Piffle. I'm here to offer you a job."

"Oh yeah? Working for you?"

"No," Mister Dark said. "Working for Mastercorp."

Vesuvia stared, positively vexed. "Mastercorp?"

"Who do you think owns all this? Who do you think *allowed* you to torment the Lanes and pursue the eighth continent? It was us, all along."

"Why would I want to work for you? I already own a billion-dollar company."

"Mastercorp is a trillion-dollar company. We make Condo Corp look like a used-sock emporium. Bargain basement. With us, think of all the marvelous things you could do, Vesuvia. Devastate landscapes. Destroy the lives of anyone who dares question you or looks at you funny. Suck every last drop of blood from the earth."

"So what?" she asked, but she found herself falling into Mister Dark's hypnotic stare.

"With our help, you could obliterate those pathetic Lanes once and for all."

Vesuvia's eyes widened. "Where do I sign?"

"Excellent!" A woman's voice said. Vesuvia had not known she was there. "I knew you would see it our way."

A shadowy figure stepped out of the darkness and into the light. She wore the same black uniform as the soldiers. Her perfect blond hair was smoothed flat against her head.

Vesuvia's mouth hung open wider than Chompedo's. "Mom?"

MATT LONDON (http://themattlondon.com) is a writer, video game designer, and avid recycler who has published short fiction and articles about movies, TV, video games, and other nerdy stuff. Matt is a graduate of the Clarion Writers' Workshop, and studied computers, cameras, rockets, and robots at New York University. When not investigating lost civilizations, Matt explores the mysterious island where he lives—Manhattan.

Find out more at

8THCONTINENTBOOKS.COM